THE DEVILS THAT HAVE COME TO STAY

THE
DEVILS
THAT HAVE
COME TO
STAY

PAMELA
DIFRANCESCO

MEDALLION
P R E S S
Medallion Press, Inc.

Printed in USA

For Mya Adriene and Sarah

Published 2015 by Medallion Press, Inc.
The MEDALLION PRESS LOGO
is a registered trademark of Medallion Press, Inc.

Copyright © 2015 by Pamela DiFrancesco
Cover design by Michal Wlos
Edited by Lorie Popp Jones

Typeset in Adobe Garamond Pro
Printed in the United States of America

ISBN # 978-160542581-8
10 9 8 7 6 5 4 3 2 1

First Edition

ACKNOWLEDGMENTS

Thanks go out to many people who made this book possible. Sarah Baker for being my loudest and most constant cheerleader, among other things. Vicki Stone and Stanley Robert Cox from the Tuolumne Band of Me-Wuk Indians, who graciously agreed to read for historical accuracy of the Me-Wuk character in the novel. Emily Steele for choosing this piece for publication and Lorie Jones for her amazing editing work. Joselin Linder, Mary Adkins, Ilise Carter, Nicole Solomon, Alia Phibes, Sam Ritchie, Joanne Solomon, Christine Clarke, and Kate Tellers: the wonderful people of my writing group who read an earlier draft and offered advice and guidance. Jad Abdallah and Shannon Hughes for their reading and suggestions. Ron Kuby for reducing my fear of sirens. Edward Ackerman and Andrew Petonak for giving me confidence in my writing when I needed it most. Siddhartha Deb for the writing assignment that provided the first five pages of this novel. Frank Jones for the use of his lovely home in which much of this novel was written. Jim Jarmusch, Alejandro Jodorowsky, and Cormac McCarthy for "blazing the trail," so to speak. Susan Lee Johnson, Eugene Conrotto, David W. Jackson, C. Hart Merriam, and Charles Ross Parke, who all wrote books invaluable to my research.

Finally, I thank my beloved partner in life and art, Mya Adriene Byrne. She was the first set of eyes on my earliest draft, picked up on details like the year in which cigarettes became popularized that I might not have thought of without her, and offered me the support and sometimes kick in the butt I needed to keep writing this novel. Her daily work to create a better world gives me hope; the love she brings to my life sustains me.

DECEMBER 21, 1848

With Joanna away, sleep does not come easily. I lay awake in bed, thinking over days, words, but nothing becomes clear. I have never seen much use in words. I hear men tell stories, stake claims, make plans, and the next day see those men right where they were the day before, all their words forgotten, having created nothing. There is something to this world that makes words fail.

The reason I write these words now is that something is happening. I cannot comprehend it, and I dare not trouble Joanna with it. I am not sure what this something is, but it seems to have started in words. Whispers. Rumors. Threats. I can't say I didn't hear someone whisper, "Ruined." I heard the long, quiet syllable of "rush" and felt the terrifying loosening that comes with it.

One day, when I was crossing the town square, I heard a language that had never before touched my ears. Not white and not the mutterings of Indians. Something full of clucks like a chicken and sounds that rose above the way people talk. When I looked, I saw no face to match it, just the faces

I see every day. The change began in these sounds, and now it has gone further. It seems the only way to understand it is by putting my own words around it.

It was two days ago that the Indian walked in and sat down in front of me. I can say it was something I never expected, not here, and from the way the men put their cards and glasses down, they must not have expected it, either.

He looked like an Indian, only different. His hair was full of knots and tangles as thick as a rope. His dark skin was red with some sort of bumps, several of them open and oozing at the center. The largest open lesion was in the middle of his forehead between his eyebrows. I kept looking into it instead of his eyes, which were swollen around the edges with the bumps. I suppose it was not so strange a place to rest my eyes, with how bad the rest of his face looked, but the strange thing was that I began to feel as if the wound was staring back.

—Barkeeper don't take feathers and beads, said George, who was closest to the Indian.

The Indian turned to look at George. There was something defiant about him, sick and unhappy as he appeared. It wasn't his stature. He was short, as are the local Indians, the Diggers—a bit bigger than an older child. It was the way he held himself. Aloof. A bitter sort of remove you'd need to walk into a place where the men would as soon kill you as say hello.

George didn't look away, but he didn't move any closer to the Indian. I thought that by now George would have drawn his gun, but I suppose he didn't want to drag a dead, diseased Indian out of the saloon any more than I did.

—Quiet, George, I said. I took down a cracked glass and poured the Indian some whisky.

The Indian took his time working on the drink. His hand shook, and he didn't say anything.

The whole saloon was silent. Then someone, maybe George, coughed.

—You might be getting sick in the lights, George, said a man we call Smithy.

With the quiet broken a bit, I knew there wasn't going to be any trouble. I moved down the bar and watched John and Daniel play cards. Every now and again I shifted my gaze to the Indian. He remained quiet, somber, staring down at his drink as if it held those secrets only Indians think they can see. At one point, he raised his hand to his chin and, slowly, as if against great resistance, ran it from his right cheek, across his mouth, to the left cheek. Once, as I watched, a feather dislodged itself from the mess of his hair and seesawed in the air before falling to the bar.

I looked up some time later, and the seat was empty.

—Goddamn Injun left a goddamn mess, George called.

With a piece of rag, I walked to where the Indian had sat, expecting spilled whisky. Instead, I saw more than a dozen feathers scattered around the floor. I tried to picture the Indian, and it seemed he had not had that many feathers anywhere on his person. But I could have been wrong. I went to get the broom.

—Like a dead angel sat there, Daniel said, seeing the mess.

—You're drunk. Shut your mouth.

That night, after all the men had gone home and the saloon was closed, quiet, and dark, I broke up the stool the Indian had sat on and burned it out back. I threw the feathers into the modest blaze, too, though I was tempted to keep one.

DECEMBER 27, 1848

After the incident of the Indian, the days passed without event, and the saloon once again became my sanctuary. When I consider the disagreements, the drunken men, and the long hours, the word "sanctuary" seems a strange choice, and yet I let it stand.

The saloon is a world where everything has an order, a world unlike the one outside its doors. The cracked glasses for strangers and for men who always break glasses will forever be on the left half of the shelf behind the bar. The good glasses will always be on the right and go to the less rowdy regulars. The bottles will always be in order from least to most expensive, except for when it is so busy I lose track of order. John and Daniel will play cards night after night at the table by the door, mostly quietly, sometimes cursing one another. George will unerringly show up at four o'clock and drink for hours before speaking. Smithy will drink until he sings old songs into his whisky glass. These are things I can count on.

The first night after the Indian came, the men were

restless. They always turn to see who is coming in every time the door opens, but that night they did so with quick jerks of their necks like they were having spasms. As they turned their heads back to their primary positions, some of them had a look of guilt in their eyes.

By the second night, the men talked of the incident with bravado they had not had two nights before.

—Damn Injun, George said. —I'd like to see him again. Whatever's sick won't be the thing that kills him if I do. He then scratched his long beard and moved on to other subjects.

The men had all but forgotten the Indian when the Stranger showed up. Strangers come and go infrequently at the saloon, but when they do they stop by while doing a stint at the mills; they come through town traveling north and spread word of the latest place the ore has been found. I listen to their stories with a poker face and expect never to see or hear from them again. But this stranger was different. He burst through the door, making some of the men jump. Perhaps they had not forgotten the Indian after all.

The Stranger's gun was drawn, glinting dull steel in the dim of the saloon. The way he walked, a wobble in his legs at the knee joints, told me he had been drinking for some time. His lips drew back in a snarl, and I noticed the yellow shimmer of a mouthful of gold teeth.

—You best state your purpose with that gun, George said, standing and reaching for his own.

—I don't mean any man any harm. I'm looking for an Injun. Did any of you see an Injun come through here a few days back? Looking all sick and wrong?

The men stared at him.

—What's that information worth to you? George asked.

I pretended to polish a glass. I find it is best to remain calm even when the men cannot.

—Quite a sight if I find him, the Stranger said. —I'm following him from the north. Leaves a trail of feathers everywhere he goes. That's how I know he's been this way. Injun stole a pile of gold from me. Any man who helps me find him stands to gain.

George laughed behind his beard. —I ain't never given out information on a maybe.

The Stranger's lips got tight, covering his gold teeth. He tipped his hat back and turned to the other men. His face was red and sweaty, as if the drinking he had done earlier had been hard work. —I suppose all the rest of you want to see some savage Injun run off with a decent man's gold as well?

No one spoke, just looked at him above their glasses and cards.

The Stranger waved his gun towards the men.

George had fully drawn his gun by this point. —No one here has any love for Injuns, any more than they do for men waving guns in their faces. I think you best leave before one of these guns gets used.

Slowly, one by one, the men at the bar put their cards and drinks down and drew their guns.

I have a gun of my own—a Colt Paterson percussion revolver with a mother-of-pearl handle—under the shelf that holds the bottles of whisky. I never wanted that gun, but my wife insisted I keep it behind the bar. At times it glimmers at me as if with some terrible certainty, calling for me to pick it up. But I do not. And I did not then. I continued to polish that glass until it shone like the Stranger's teeth.

The Stranger saw he was outnumbered. He stumbled backwards towards the door. He lowered his gun as if it weighed too much for him to hold any longer. Taking it in his palm, he offered his thin wrists to the ceiling of the saloon.

—They've taken everything, he shouted. Tendons stood out in his neck as he cast his eyes and chin upwards. — What can a man have that they don't take away? How can a man be expected to lose everything to these goddamn monsters and just take and take it?

His chest heaving with the heat of his declaration, he kicked the door behind him open and stepped away from the steady line of steel guns winking at him in the musty air of the saloon. The door closed behind him.

When a few moments had passed, the men slowly put their guns back in their belts.

JANUARY 3, 1849

The night after the Stranger came into the bar, I could not sleep. At times, when Joanna is here, we walk through the woods late at night, finding our way through the roots and rocks to the spot in which I fish, the spot where we met years ago. The early morning we met, I had my fishing line in the water, waiting for the touch on the line, the light tug that would signal that I had caught something. Instead, I felt a touch on my elbow. I turned and saw the woman who would become my wife.

I supposed the effect was reached by a combination of moonlight and rippling water, but I could have sworn I glimpsed a wave of silver dance across her neck. Sometimes, when she is asleep in bed at night, I look at what the lovely neck has become—older, with softer muscle, the skin a labyrinth of wrinkles. It is no longer the austere white and silver I saw that morning.

—You're out early for a young lady, I said, though in these parts it was never very safe for a young lady to be about.

—There's something on your line, she replied.

She was right. I fought for only a few moments before I pulled the twisting and glistening fish from the water.

I yanked my line in and cut it. The fish lay wriggling and gasping between us, but for all its metallic dancing, the light of the moon once again focused on the lady.

—It's late for anyone to be out. Joanna spoke to my statement from before.

—I can't sleep some nights, I said. —It's a good fishing spot.

The water was black. The fish was silver. Its wriggling had almost stopped. It might be dead now, no matter what, I thought, but I removed the hook from its mouth and threw it back into the water. We watched as it caught its bearings and swam away. And that is how I met my wife many years ago.

But Joanna has been gone for months. I don't know if she will come back. Her letters grow darker and stranger, and I wonder where this quality comes from—her, me, or the world around us.

Thoughts of Joanna swirled through my mind as I rose from bed. On such a night, my restlessness would have woken her, and we would have walked by the stream. It was where I chose to go alone, stepping over the cold mud created by a steady rain that had only recently cleared.

I walked through the trees to the clear, low sound of the creek. The area where I reside is replete with creeks, and all of them sound the same except this one. Maybe it is just because I consider this one as belonging to Joanna and me that I imagine it sounds singular. As I approached it, I could hear heartbeats, low and calm. I could almost hear singing.

Strange, however, that as I moved nearer the water, I thought the heartbeats sounded sluggish, like a sick man's. When flashes of the stream appeared through the trees, its silver looked dimmed. Chalking up these differences to my own eyes and ears, I readied my fishing pole.

I cast out and stood with my line in the water for some time, trying to regulate the heartbeat of the stream with my attention to its rhythm. Slow and inconsistent as it was, it lulled me into a trance that only the eventual bite of a fish jarred me from. I pulled on the line, and it was not long before I felt the fish loosen from the trap of the water in one last tug.

I stood staring in horror.

I had expected the fish to be silver or black or the darkest blue of the post-sunset sky. By off chance, I'd expected the white of pale fish that swim in depths, feeding off death. But no. The fish the black water had released shone like the ore of which I have heard so many stories. Pure gold. It flopped on the ground, its impending death never for a moment dulling its precious sheen.

But the horror had only begun. The heartbeat of the water seemed to sputter and stop. The motion of the creek seemed to slow. My own heart may have skipped a beat as the water froze in its progress. I looked down at the dead fish as the creek started to bubble.

I closed my eyes. When I opened them again, the edges of the creek were filled with the dull glint of tarnished silver. The silver moved and rippled like the slow motion of the wheels and pistons of long trains as they pull into stations.

The edge of the creek was lined with dead fish. Their eyes were white and milky against the black of the night water. I stood staring, trying to comprehend what could have happened. No understanding came to me.

After staring for several moments, I cut my line, leaving the gold fish near the banks of the stream. As I turned to walk home, I saw something white in the mud. A single white feather trampled by my boots.

And now I sit here, straining to find the words to describe what could have happened that night. "Unholy" occurs to me, but it does not seem right to mention holiness in a scene it has no part in. "Ungodly" is a problem, too, not because I don't believe God creates the terror in this world, but because that night wasn't even the kind of terror I think God capable of casting out. It seems any undoing of a positive word cannot match the destruction I have seen. So this again is where words cannot touch the horror of what I cannot begin to understand. This is where the notion of telling fails me as it has failed me before, leaving me cold and staring without comprehension.

There will be no sleep tonight.

My dear,

I write these words with struggle. I wish I could tell you that all is well, that Mother is thriving, that I myself am untroubled, and that Coloma is the town we knew from the trips to visit my family. But she is not, I am not, and it certainly is not.

The family has become skittish, unrecognizable. Father, once so content to work his fields however little they yielded each year, has succumbed to the notion that his days as a farmer are over, and the land is beyond hope. Nathaniel and Mary argue late into the night, and sometimes they are so loud that the baby wakes and adds her cries to their angry voices. Perhaps because of these nocturnal awakenings, little Josephine, who used to be the picture of health and radiance, has turned into an irate, sullen child. Her blonde hair has begun to shade itself darker, not a light brown, as could be expected, but coal black. Each day as Mary and I run a brush through it, a new dark patch appears. Stephen has abandoned all hope, and, as I write this, he packs his clothes, Grandfather's watch, and Grandmother's silver serving tray. He says the only way out is to go farther north and escape the devils that have come to stay.

Mother's illness troubles us all more and more. The doctor cannot understand it and is calling it a "nervous health crisis." This phrase means little to us, and the doctor seems unable to describe it in a way we can understand. We are left to glean knowledge of her condition from what she says and what we observe. The information grows more disturbing daily. She thinks the water from the well bad, though the rest of us drink it regularly to no trouble. She rises from bed only infrequently, which means we must keep the fire burning all day to warm her. She cries in the night that the sparks burn her, though the rest of us see no sparks near her. We have moved her bed into the kitchen across from the woodstove, but her complaints of burns are punctuated by her insistence that a frigid cold is seeping into her bones. Oh, my dear, if you were here, perhaps you could make sense of this.

Father maintains, despite his lost hope for his land, that Mother will recover. Watching her ruined frame writhing from flame and cold, I find this hope beyond reason. If only I could find some faith left inside my own thinning body and languishing mind. As it is, all I see is ruin. I watch green branches wither and die.

John Sutter's land has fared worse than Father's. As you know, Sutter's land was where the cursed ore was first found. We never bore any love for Sutter, but now, as all his men have abandoned their work and the land lies ravaged, we understand that we never bore him the malice his fate bespeaks.

One rare day when Mother was well enough to eat, our spirits lifted, and Mary and I took little Josephine walking. We thought to take her to the golden fields of the Sutter place, but when we arrived we found huge pits dug in the ground and dirt piled high above them. The river was murky and dark, filled with loosened silt, old metal, and the Lord prevents me from saying what else. It was as if the whole place had been ravaged by beasts. Beasts they must have been to do such things to a land that was once the work of God's very hands.

Not all the mill hands were gone. Over by a pit of dirt, we spied five men toiling to fill a hole. Their efforts seemed strained, and as we walked closer to them, we saw why. These toiling men had been battered by some force unknown to us— one man was missing all the fingers from one hand and managed to shovel weakly with the other; one's face was distorted from pain and rage while his limbs fluttered like wings that can no longer fly; still a third had shoulders tilted at a steep angle, one high and one low, and dragged half his body behind him. We did not stay to gaze upon the other two men.

Sutter's place, Father's farm, and all of Coloma are empty but for shades of people that once dwelt there. It seems that after the initial rush, after the beasts came and took everything they could use, all that is left for the rest of us is that which bears no value. In the main streets of Coloma, the general store appears bent. Its windows have been broken and all the goods taken. Every now and again, a lone elderly man or woman can be seen tottering, bucket in hand, to the well.

But other images come into view, too. One day, I saw a man in a suit and tie setting up a machine to record visual evidence. For a moment, I did not see clearly and almost thought it a wonder, the newness that takes the place of the old, familiar, and loved. Then my vision cleared, and I saw that even the expensive machine was a sign of the ruin.

I do not know when I will return to you, my dear, return to our quiet life—our little home, the saloon, our infrequent but treasured walks by the stream. I wish you to know that I adore that life, and I would have it back in an instant, if only it were possible. Why is it that tonight, as I write you by the flickering light of this candle alongside Mother's forlorn moan, it seems impossible?

With all my love,
Joanna

JANUARY 12, 1849

As I read Joanna's last letter, my hands shook. The paper moved up and down with them, lodging the words deep in my mind. Perhaps my eyes widened, for everything around me seemed bright and wet, shimmering as if it were a painting that was not yet dry. Each sound might have marked the onset of an earth-ending catastrophe, an earthquake or a gargantuan ocean wave.

I began at once to write back to her, to try to pen some sort of comfort or assurance. Nothing came. I could not find a word to undo the smallest bit of what she had told me. While her letter had carried the truth and terror of the world around her, mine would just be vagueness—something as inconsistent and insubstantial as the thoughts of "comfort" or "hope."

Sleep, which had come so infrequently before, abandoned me entirely. I spent the nights wandering—not fishing, not hiking, just walking through the trees and brush and mud with no destination. Most nights, the trees lurked over me, frightening wraiths. Joanna's letter haunted my mind.

Instead of the comforting heartbeat of the stream, I heard her mother's moans.

Last night, I decided to walk to the north to avoid the stream and the trees. I planned to go to a field that lies in a clearing, somewhere I could rest and clear my mind. Only when I arrived, I found the strangest sight yet.

At first glance, I thought I had happened across a girl dancing in the moonlight. The lithe figure, shrouded partially in white, moved gracefully in a swirling pattern, its arms outstretched. Then the trance of the moonlight left me, and I could see that the figure had but one arm outstretched, and small, glittering pieces were falling from its hand. A strange song was coming from its throat. I couldn't make it out. It didn't sound like anything I've ever heard before, and behind the bar as I usually am, I have heard many things.

I stepped closer and realized that the figure was not a woman but a man with long, dark hair, knotted and twisted, naked but for a cloth around his waist. I took another step and noticed his skin was not smooth and soft, as I had first assumed, but marked with sickness. It was the Indian.

Upon seeing me, he stopped his bizarre dance. His gaze fell upon me. Again, as at the saloon, he looked like he was holding himself above me. —Are you a messenger of the white man who has set out to kill me?

For a moment I said nothing. I knew he was the kind of Indian that resides here in the hills and coast, the kind that does not love violence. But still I feared he might do me harm, draw some Indian's weapon. I stood stock-still.

He did not move, either, but regarded me calmly. He raised his hand and ran it across the lower half of his face, contemplating me.

—I'm a messenger of no one, I said. —I come here for myself.

The Indian studied me, possibly thinking I was about to pull a white man's weapon from my clothes. When he saw that I had no such intentions, he put his hand into the pouch at his side and resumed his dance. Though he looked like he was swirling in some seed-gathering ceremony, he was scattering. And though what he was scattering was sometimes as small as seeds, it was far more precious by most accounts. It was gold.

The Indian scattered gold for several minutes. As some fell at my feet, I felt the urge to gather it. But as I went to my knees to pick it up, the moist ground had already begun to absorb it like a dry sponge taking in water. Before I could take a single piece, it was swallowed by the earth.

I clawed at the ground, thinking the disappearance was perhaps a trick of the moonlight. But no. While mud clung to my fingers and I unearthed a few small stones, I found that the gold was completely gone. Something could not exist in one moment and be gone the next. I dug frantically. The wet earth shifted beneath the demands of my hands. It shone in the moonlight and sucked at my skin. For a second, a crack appeared in the logic of the night around me. Was this earth, were those trees, was that moon, were the Indian and I of the four elements of this reality or of the ether? I did not feel in any position to answer that question.

I looked up at the Indian, my mouth working to express what I could hardly fathom. I tried to speak of disappearance, but what had happened carried a sickening sense that the utterance could not touch.

—It is best not to gather what's been stolen from the earth in the first place, he told me.

His simple phrase seemed to convey something more. The hollow echoes of his strange words sounded where my own would not. We were speaking of different worlds, and his intonations both confused and satisfied me. I stilled my grasping hand and rested it in the tender stalks of grass. Each one of them was simple and real beneath my muddy hand. My chest rose and fell as I waited for him to say more. But no more came.

I had many questions, and there in the darkness, I began asking them. —How do you speak English so well? The other Indians I can barely understand.

The Indian laughed, and I could see in the way he threw back his head that he had not always been the sad, sick man I met in my saloon, looking for answers in a glass of whisky. His defiance flashed again in the night, like a late-rising star.

—That is what concerns this white man? he said. —Then let me tell you: I am a storyteller. It benefits a storyteller to speak many tongues.

—Did you steal that stranger's gold?

—How can I steal what's already been stolen?

—Stolen from who?

—Stolen from the earth. Stolen and poisoned.

I thought of the river full of dead fish. But here, the gold had disappeared into the mud, sinking and vanishing. Here and gone. A shudder echoed through a place deep inside me.

—Gold and white men make strange companions, he went on. —It seems the more gold a white man sees, the less value he is able to see in anything besides gold. There is much value in this land I travel, but all white men can see is shiny rocks.

—Where do you travel? I asked.

—I have made many circles in my life, but this is my biggest, and I believe it will be my last. No matter how I empty my bag of gold, it seems full. No matter how many feathers fall behind me, there seems more to fall. It seems Coyote has me trapped in one of his games. Perhaps if I can make it back to where the gold came from, my bag will empty, and the last feather will fall. I have traveled from near the place you men call Sutter's Fort, and I am returning there.

I froze. Sutter's Fort is near where Joanna is staying. On the nights when I do sleep, the fields of Sutter's Fort haunt my dreams. As I slumber, they roll and stretch, reaching far past the boundaries that constrain them in reality. They move like the smoke that creeps quietly from a fire and, as the fire grows, darkens the whole sky.

Before I knew the words coming out of my mouth, I said, —I'm starting for Coloma tonight.

I thought of the saloon, empty and abandoned, my place of sanctuary just another outdated temple like they say the Indians in the south left behind. Then I thought of my wife, alone, listening to her mother's moans in the night. I knew what I had said was right.

I looked to the Indian. In the moonlight, I could almost ignore the sickness that was so apparent on his skin and see him as fair as he once must have been, muscled, lean, his hair shining and flying. Again he moved his hand across his sick face, from one ruined cheek to the other, bringing me back to the reality of the sickness there.

—And would a white man like you share the road to Coloma with a sick Indian thief? He smiled.

I thought of that gold fish. Of the gold sinking into the earth as I tried to pick it up. Of the flash of gold teeth above the dull metal gun when the Stranger burst into my saloon. I thought of other things, too, things buried deeply in time and my mind, things that I struggle on my worst days to hold down.

—A white man like me would.

The Indian walked to the edge of the field where his clothes of fur and white cloth were. He dressed in what seemed like a strange ceremony, holding them out before him and shaking the earth from them, all the while singing his lilting song. At times, the song rose to the tops of the trees at the edges of the clearing, and at other times, it swung down to the ground that had absorbed the gold.

I told the Indian I needed to return to my rooms to pack. He told me he would meet me along the road.

The walk home seemed to take less time than the walk to the field. I felt lighter, as if I walked in bare feet instead of heavy boots. Before long, I found myself opening the outside door, passing the door that led to the saloon, and climbing the stairs to my quiet rooms.

I passed through the living quarters to the bedroom at the back. There was a woolen blanket on my and Joanna's marriage bed that I took and folded. In the center of it, I placed this journal and the gun I keep behind the bar when the saloon is open. I had promised myself long ago that I would never use that gun, but it seemed foolish to leave it behind now. I put these things, along with some clothes and money, into a sack, which I slung over my shoulder.

With these necessities packed, I stepped around the bed and to the far wall, where a window sat partially open. I only intended to close it, but as I neared it, I looked down to the clear view of the road below. Not a soul traveled it. I lamented the fact that I would not be able to call upon anyone to say good-bye at this hour but then realized there was no one to whom I wished to say good-bye. I took my hands off the cool glass and closed the window.

As I stood alone, I felt much the same as I had when I thought of the empty saloon. Soon somber dust would settle over everything. I might never see these rooms again. Soon I would place a board across my door and nail it shut, keeping the life I was leaving behind sealed inside.

But there was no time to linger on such sentiments. I strode to the front room and closed the door to my home behind me.

And that was how my journey began.

JANUARY 25, 1849

The Indian and I have traveled for days, or rather, for many nights. I felt it would be best for us to take this nocturnal course as the Indian said the Stranger would likely be in pursuit.

The Indian protested at first. —Only the least desirable creatures travel at night, he said. —Kah'-kool, the raven, the spirits, the underworld people.

But I insisted, and he relented.

Our first day began as the sun went down. I packed up our camp. Sleeping by day allows us to let the fire die as we slumber, so I had to build a new one after I folded my blanket and returned it to the pack. While I did this, the Indian took a leather pouch from around his neck and extracted a small leaf, which he then ate.

—What's that? I asked.

—It will help me find bigger prey.

The Indian returned later with a dead animal about the size of a cat. As he carried it almost lovingly in the crook of one arm, he paused every now and then to lean to one side and vomit. He had barely wiped the vomit from his lips before he started to speak about Indian things that I do not understand.

—Ah-ha'-le, Coyote, is after me again. The marks on my skin are his bite wounds. The gold in my pouch is his shit, he said, wiping the vomit from his lips.

The second morning, the Indian did not eat his strange intoxicant and returned to camp with acorns and small, dead prey like mice and squirrels. He crushed the former with the latter, and we ate a sort of porridge of them. It was not something I was accustomed to or even liked, but it was what we had, and I was grateful for it. Both mornings, we cooked in a metal bowl I brought and ate together from it. I could taste nothing but the metal.

After we ate our after-sunset breakfast, we walked. We have used no map yet, and I do not suspect we will. When I asked the Indian about this, he said to follow the direction I felt was most worthy. However, each night he set off to the northwest, judging by where the sun has set. For the first few nights, I followed him until he disappeared. One night, I was close enough, and I watched the feathers fall from his hair and clothes. I swore I would observe closely, to see how it was possible that so many fell from him. But when one fell, I watched it tumble to the earth and lost track of his person. By the time I looked up, he had disappeared and I had only the trail of feathers to follow.

We walked the whole night through. The land, which once seemed familiar to me, was no longer so. It may have been, in part, due to traveling in darkness, but the trees we walked through seemed like streaks of phosphorus from the ground to the sky. Their white bark stood out against the blackness of the cosmos. At one point, when the Indian was close by, I told him as much. He did not look surprised.

—So early on this journey, and already you see the spirits of things, he said.

I told him I could see nothing good about it. All I have ever wished for was the land and the trees and the world around me to be as solid and comforting as I once found them. Even as my relationship to the earth has changed, as I have spent more time inside behind a bar than out, glimpses of that earth have always comforted me, made me sure of quiet and growth and a natural progression. This new world I am traveling, full of ghosts and coyotes, is no more comforting than the terrifying glimmer of the world this gold fever is bringing.

—The world changes, the Indian replied. —I have always done my best not to hurt it during these changes while it is exposed.

The Indian and I always meet on the trail just before dawn. I suspect he waits for me and that otherwise I would never find him. He insists on camping in a place near water, as he has the habit of bathing ritualistically after each dawn. The relief of dawn, with the orange sun dispersing the spirits of the night, is too great to tell.

As we make camp at dawn, the Indian tells stories. He seems to do it as a matter of course. After the long night of walking and solitude, his words are a comfort, no matter how little I understand them. Most of the stories are about Coyote, of whom he speaks frequently. One of them

was about how Coyote attempted to steal the sun. He tied
a string to it and tried to pull it out of the heavens. But no
matter how hard he pulled, the sun just rolled around in the
sky. The stubborn Coyote wouldn't give up, and now day
and night he pulls the sun from east to west.

Then the Indian told the oddest part of the tale. —And
at times, I follow Coyote, laughing. That is what wakes the
birds in the trees up and makes them sing—my laughter.

The Indian figures himself into many of his stories.
One day I will have to ask him if this is what a storyteller is
supposed to do.

JANUARY 27, 1849

This evening the Indian left camp and did not come back. I sat waiting for him as the sun sank lower and lower in the sky, leaving an orange glow to the west that lessened until it was finally nothing. The night deepened into blue, and stars appeared in the sky with gaps of darkness between them. I waited and waited. He was gone. I could not even find his trail of feathers.

I set out from camp alone and shortly came across another camp. I watched from between the trees. The four men were settling in for the evening. Three of them wore felt hats whose brims had not yet been beaten down by the rain and wind and sun. One wore all leather, from his boots to his hat, and it was easy to see from the way he directed the others that he was the leader of the group.

I watched through the trees as they unpacked their mules and horses, wondering if I should speak to them. I watched as they started a campfire and set a small pot on three legs above it. From the still-shining quality of their cooking materials, I surmised they were new in the search for gold. I have known such men to be likely to accept any-thing that comes by them. I made my way through the trees.

—Where are you men headed? I called by way of greeting.

The four men wheeled around at once to face me, and one man's new hat fell off his head to the ground.

—I'd ask the same question of you, said the one in leather.

—I am on the trail to Sutter's Fort, I said.

—Aw, said the man whose hat had fallen off. —You're seeking your fortune like the rest of us.

—Yes, I suppose I am just like you.

I had been correct about their ready acceptance. The men got back to making camp as if I wasn't even there and fell into talking about what they would do with their for-tunes. I had heard the excited babble before, but this time I listened to it more closely.

—I'm gonna marry my sweetheart in Austin when I find my gold. I'll build us a house, and we'll have a pack of children.

—I'll find my fortune but not for no woman.

—Yeah, what do you want it for, then?

—A house for my ma and pa, the first man replied.

—I'd take your ma over any old woman, too, another man shouted.

The man who wanted to buy his parents a house took the statement in good humor, and he and the man who'd commented on it began to wrestle near where the man in the leather was stoking the fire. It was a great show of strength, with both men grabbing and grappling at one another. Finally, the man who wanted to build the house picked the other one up, flung him over his shoulder, and walked in circles.

—Aw, let me down! Let me down! yelled the hapless victim, thrusting his arms out as if to find something to grab onto.

I felt a sense of lightness come over me as I helped the man in leather feed sticks to the fire. It had been some time since I was around men who were joyous.

In the middle of this joy, I remembered Joanna's letter. I froze while carrying sticks to the fire pit. I tried to swallow the fear that made itself known as a lump in my throat. These men had no idea what they were headed for in the north, in the fields they believed lined with gold.

With this thought in mind, I could not watch their antics. Then it grew difficult to even look at their faces. The youngest, no more than twenty, still had the round, unmarred cheeks of a child. As he smiled and laughed, I imagined those cheeks growing thinner and thinner, hollowing out until his face was just yellow flesh drawn tight over brittle skull. I pictured the rest of his body swelling and then the skin tearing, exposing the pink and raw beneath. He would find death and ruin, I was sure.

My stomach tightened. I did not know why I cared about the fate of this young man or had envisioned his demise so clearly. But it shook me in ways that I hadn't thought possible a few days before. I have seen much from behind the bar at my saloon and even more in the days before that, before Joanna came into my life. But suddenly, out in this open sky and darkness, my grim vision meant more than many real events I'd born witness to.

I paced the camp quietly after that, saying little. The men were undaunted by anything, continuing their jokes and boisterousness. They invited me to stay for dinner, and I accepted. Soon bacon brought with them from whatever outpost they'd just arrived from was sizzling over that spider pan, cracking and popping along with the noise of the fire. The men brought forth loaves of sourdough bread. The man in leather set coffee boiling on the fire, for which they even had a bit of sugar. We sat down to dinner no more than an hour later, and it was more palatable than anything I'd eaten with the Indian.

After the meal, one of the men went to his belongings and took out a banjo. The youngest sang a low, haunting song about a girl who'd married a man who didn't love her and how unhappy she was.

> *Alas, my love, he wanders.*
> *Alas, he goes astray.*
> *Alas, I rue my wedding bells*
> *With each lone passing day.*
> *Each lone passing day.*

I wanted to ask where he knew it from, but he looked away after he finished, and I never did ask.

Not long after the song was done, I stood to leave. I was sorry to be going, but night had deepened, and I had to move along.

JANUARY 28, 1849

Back on my own, food is scarce. A part of me wants to hunt. In the days past, days before I met my Joanna, I moved among the trees and over fields with my gun, trapping and killing, marking myself with the musk of animals, trying to blend into the wilderness. I moved alone, my company the animals I tracked and took the lives of. But it has been many years since I have pointed a gun or taken a life in any way. Many years since the night I promised to lay down my gun for good. Here, those years do not seem so far away anymore.

I remember the blood of the animals as it would run into the ground after the kill. There were men who relished the smell and the sight of it. Those were mostly men new to the hunt, who still worked for the trapping companies, paying off their debts to them. I was never one to take pleasure like that in the kill. For me, the kill always seemed like a poor ending to a story. As soon as it happened, there was something like an absence that rang through the forest. Perhaps "absence" is not the word, for the carcass, the meat, and the pelt had weight and scent and feel to them. But perhaps "absence" *is* the right word, for as soon as the trigger was pulled and the life extinguished, the woods and the fields felt silent and hollow. My hearing, so heightened before, returned to its usual level. My sight, keen as the knife in my belt, lowered until the edges of things blurred. Perhaps the end of anything, no matter how insignificant it seems, is an absence.

It has been years since these thoughts have come to me. When I look back at the man I was then, I do not like what I see. Alone in the fields. Solitary over the hills and mountains. A mountain man, I was called. There were certainly those who envied that man. Called me free. But often I felt more trapped than the animals that had no chance against me.

And then there was Joanna. And suddenly, the memories become softer, easier to bear.

FEBRUARY 1, 1849

The Indian and I have been separated for days, and no matter how hard I look for his trail of feathers, I do not find it. I realize I am making a longer path for myself by searching for them, but I feel compelled to look. I suspect he does not want to be caught and uses some sort of Indian magic against it. Or maybe his Coyote is foiling me now and leaving him alone.

This morning, I was making camp when I heard a rustling in the trees. I turned in the direction, and I swear I saw the glint of metal.

All was quiet for a moment, and I began to relax.

Then a voice called out, —You headed north to the gold fields?

—Yes. I have come to assume that is the safest answer.

The man emerged from the trees, carrying a heavy pack on his back. He looked like any other man searching for gold in the north, and at first I didn't recognize him. Then he coughed and made a sound in his throat, his lips pulling back in a grimace. I noticed the glint of gold in his mouth.

It was the Stranger who had come into my saloon.

—You mind if I join you? I have food.

Apparently he had not seen me through his haze of drunkenness the night we met. The clothes I wore on the journey—a flannel shirt and black canvas pants—were not the clothes he would have seen me clad in at the saloon. And I had no such things as gold teeth to give away my true identity.

—Food's always a welcome thing, I said, thinking of the berries and leaves I had been eating since the Indian disappeared.

—Why are you traveling by night? he asked.

—I'm not, I lied. —I let my fire go out last night. I'm making fire for breakfast before heading out.

I began to gather sticks and logs for the fire.

The Stranger heaved his pack down on the ground. He looked calmer today but just as exhausted as that day in the bar. His eyes, which had burned and raged out of his pale face in the saloon, were dark and set deep in his face, almost peaceful. In the saloon his face had seemed sharp with anger, but this morning, it was almost a different shape— broader and flatter. As if he were another man altogether. It surprised me a bit and made me wonder if perhaps he was not the man I had seen that night. But I know men can have many faces.

—Are you headed north to make your fortune? I asked.

—I am headed north, yes, he said.

Sober, he was quiet but no less determined. Some fire still glowed deep inside him, but it was closed off, like his gold teeth were hidden when his mouth was shut. His face was wrinkled underneath a shelf of heavy dark eyebrows. He was about my age, but as he rolled up his sleeves to help me with the fire, I saw that beneath the coarse dark hair of his arms, his skin was wrinkled and loose. There was not much muscle to speak of. I wondered how he had managed to frighten us in the bar.

Knowing more than he thought I knew, I pressed him for answers. —What form does your fortune take? The gold mine does?

He coughed and grimaced again. He spat into the ring of stones where we were piling sticks, making teepees of larger logs. —My fortune is long gone. All that's left to get is the gold.

The Stranger laughed a bitter, dry laugh that produced another cough. He didn't speak as he pulled provisions out of his pack. I watched to make sure he didn't pull his gun. It seemed without whisky he didn't have the strength to do that. Then I saw him remove a bottle of whisky and began to worry where the meal would take us.

I built the fire, and the Stranger unpacked bread and jerky. The jerky he drew from a leather pouch. He did not seem to have the provisions that the men I had camped with a few nights before had, but he had certainly prepared himself better than I had. He took a piece of jerky and tore into it with his gold teeth. The teeth shone against the leathery matter of the meat. He extended a piece to me, and I accepted it. I chewed and chewed, remoistening the dried meat with my saliva.

I remembered his shout as he was leaving my bar. *What*

can a man have that they don't take away? How can a man be expected to lose everything to these goddamn monsters and just take and take it? I wondered what he had meant and if I could trust his words even now.

—Where did it go? I asked.

He looked at me as if I were insane. He grabbed another piece of jerky out of his bag and bit into it. He finished it before he spoke again. —Where did what go?

—Your fortune. And what do you mean, gold's not your fortune? I thought gold was everybody's fortune who's traveling north.

The Stranger drew out another piece of tough jerky, and as he worked his mouth around it, he grimaced. —I lost my fortune long before I found any gold. And now I've lost my gold. It's all been stolen.

He told me his tale, and it brought some of the dark that was dispersing in the sunrise back around us.

—I set out from Maryland when I heard the first cries of gold. Set out with my wife and my two children. Two boys, younger than they should've been to go on such a journey. But we had to get here at all costs, it seemed. So many riches to think about that no man was thinkin' straight. When I remember those times before I heard about the riches, before I got the gold fever, those were the shinin' times. Times golder than any gold when we was in our house together around a fire, happy and healthy. I had the fever, though, and I couldn't see it. Couldn't think of nothing but getting out here.

—We got on a boat, a boat advertised as a queen of the

sea. He paused to laugh his bitter laugh. —It was a barge with the decay in her hull painted over. That we made it so far on a ship like that will never cease to amaze me. But we made it down to the Panama Isthmus. It took its toll on me to see how the journey wore on my wife and my sons. They hardly ate from the sickness of being on the water. One boy got pale, and his eyes got deep in his skull and black. His gums bled, and sometimes the blood came out from between his lips. I can still remember how he looked with those dark eyes and that blood running from his mouth. Like a night creature of some sort.

—When we reached the Isthmus, though, was when the real trouble started. We was walking through the jungle, all the while the people whose boat it was promising us a big ship on the other side and from there smooth sailing to California. They found some of them southern Injuns to guide us. On the third day, the little boy, the one who'd been the sickest on the ship, falls to the ground. The ground was wet, and our boots sank in it, and all you could hear when he fell was the ground sucking at him. He starts to have a fit, his arms and legs jerking and swaying, his eyes rollin' back in his head. He comes out of it burning up. And soon the other boy is burning up, him still so small he's sucking on his mama's teat. Then she's burning' up and telling me how her neck and her back hurt. Soon they couldn't walk no more. By the end there was blood comin' from their noses and eyes. They were spitting up blood and blackness. We camped for a week, trying to save them and the others who had caught whatever it was they caught.

But nothing was going to save them.

While he spoke, he never paused in eating his jerky. Each time he finished a piece, he reached for more. It seemed there was no end to the dried meat in that bag.

—Them damn Injun guides gave it to them. I know it. My boys and my wife died in no time at all. So when I come to California, I stayed away from them Injuns as best I could. But it's hard, with men out to make money off them. Injuns pay damn near anything for white man's clothes, and they work for cheap. I made my fortune in gold; that's true enough. Then a man who worked in the fields near me, an Injun thief, took even that 'way from me. I been robbed of everything, but I'll be damned if I'll let it all go so easy.

Another piece of jerky came out of the bag. It seemed more had come out of the bag than the bag would hold. —I'll be making camp here for the day, he said.

—And I'll be traveling on.

I gathered my things, my blanket, pans. My gun, warm from the closeness to my skin, glinted at my side. As I was tucking this journal into my bag, he spread his blanket onto the ground and stretched out on it. He lay on his back, his arms behind his head. He pulled his hat down over his eyes, but as he grimaced, I could still see the sheen of metal in his mouth. It looked unnatural against his tanned skin, against the brown of the earth and the green of the trees.

—You still think you'll find your fortune? he asked.

I thought of his wife, dead and buried in some jungle. I thought of my own, lying awake at night, perhaps knowing somewhere deep in her mind that I was coming. —Yes, I do.

I do hope I will.

    —Good luck to you, then.

    I finished packing my bag and started my first walk by day since my journey began.

My dear,

The sky shades itself darker daily. Not the hard metal blue of an arriving storm nor the blue of the sky as the sun extracts its final lights, but a deeper and more unnatural shade of blue—bluer than the deep ocean, bluer than the floor of God's heavens in painted depictions. There are times when I wish I could paint the sky daily onto a canvas in its exact color to compare each day with the previous, to be sure that this observation is not an impending madness of my own. But I have only my senses to record the progression of this change. I simply must not *believe they have begun to fail me, as they have failed Mother.*

My dear, she worsens daily.

As you know, Mother has stopped eating on a normal basis. This the same woman who once cooked great dinners for all, timed to perfection, with each plate steaming on the table as members of the family walked to their seats. I compare her presiding over those full plates and trays, inviting and gracious, to the repulsion that mars her face at the smell of food now. She but drinks juice and milk and at times a sip of brandy for any pain, real or imagined. But as often as not, the liquids will spill back out from between her lips, and we will wipe them from her chin with a cloth.

The other morning we brought some food near her. We were encouraged by the lack of recoil in her expression as we cooked it and even more so when she remained unperturbed as it got nearer her person. As the bowl of nothing less benign than porridge sat before her on a low table, Mother actually closed her eyes and took in the scent through her nostrils. Something almost resembling the slightest smile played upon her lips. We were so much heartened that as Mary raised the spoon near Mother's lips, we all felt that she would take the sustenance she so dearly needs.

Then her eyes opened. Her face contorted. —Ore! she yelled. At first it was a reedy cry that made little sense to us. Then, as if fortified by the scent of the food or I can only fear what else, the cry gained strength and meaning. —Ore! The ore! The ore! I see it there!

It was a cry we had heard in the town, from people passing through and sometimes through the open windows, in the day and in the night. It was often filled with so much joy that the resounding echoes of it were as pleasant as a song's chorus or the exclamations in a child's game. As time went on and the ruin came, the joyous cry became ominous. But never had it been as ominous as when it was coming out of Mother's mouth.

She stared directly down into the bowl of wholesome white and tan porridge, crying. —The ore! The ore! It will poison me! You've poisoned me with the ore, and you're attempting to do it again! I see the ore! Glittering there, like the eyes of the Devil himself! The ore! The ore!

We each tried to reassure her, staring into her eyes and the bowl. But soon her eyes closed in some sort of pain, creasing deep furrows into her face around the closed lids. She screamed and screamed.

Sometimes in my less rational moments, such as the one I had right then and there, I wonder if Mother's logic is more clear than all of ours put together. These moments come more often for me.

With all my love,

Joanna

FEBRUARY 3, 1849

There is magic at work here, though I know not if it is sinister or benign. The Indian referred to the spirits of things. And maybe that is the best I can fit into what I see around me.

Mists cloud my path. They seem not to come from heavy air or the moisture of streams but from the very ground itself. They envelop me in the early mornings before the sun has risen, and the world shrinks to a globe of clarity around me. Beyond that is the haze of forgetfulness, of dreams. At times the fog is so thick that parts of myself slip into it. When the sun burns in the sky, the mists fall back like shadows. Yet I can still sense their waiting presence in the rocks and the trees and the earth. When the sun slips away, the mists crowd around me again.

Their cause is a mystery, but their effect is clear enough. I stumble and lose my way. I breathe their chill into my body. I take their outward disorientation and carry it inside.

As I walk, I picture a flame. A candle. I imagine it cutting through the mists. Perhaps it does not lead me as straight and true as I would hope through the vague, swirling world, but follow it I do.

FEBRUARY 10, 1849

There is blood on this path. I thought I understood the blood of this world all too well, but I see now that I have never understood it like I understand it today. It drenches the earth around me. As I write, my hands shake.

I traveled more days alone, free from a path, free from others. In the mists, I have circled and found myself in the place I have started. I have foraged for the leaves and fruits the world around me bears. I have heard the animals break sticks and shift rocks as they run out of my way. I have despaired of ever finding the Indian or his path again. At times, I would have even welcomed the Stranger. Only today when I found others did I recall how the presence of men can make the thought of being alone and lost preferable.

The fog cleared at dawn. It seemed absent in a way it has not for some time. I thought that a good omen as I walked. My path was clear. I did not know how wrong I was.

I smelled the presence of others first in the wafting, rising aroma of a campfire. After the first whiff of burning cedar, the lighter smells of cooking came to me. I lost myself in the scents as I would in a garden of aromatic flowers. I caught hints of roasting meat, of cooking vegetables. I had eaten nothing warm or cooked in days, and I swore to myself that I would befriend whoever was tending that fire, no matter if they were demons condemned by the Lord Himself. Thinking back on this now, I laugh grimly.

I stumbled over the ground. The sun was directly overhead in its noontime stance, and I was suddenly unsure if I was traveling north, south, east, or west. All I knew was that my destination was whatever semblance of civilization lay around the fire ahead of me.

It was then that I heard the screams.

There were two kinds of shouts echoing through the trees. There were high-pitched screams of terror. Of surprise. Then there were lower, more guttural cries. The cries of a human being reduced to his most animal form and emitting cries not in horror at such debasement but in the joy of it. These screams were snarls that reverberated with lust and the pleasure derived from misery.

I stumbled faster, then ran in the direction of the camp before me. I saw the roaring fire, flickering between the trees. It leapt up gracefully and soundlessly as I was sure it had in the moments before the screaming began. That it carried on in so slow and elegant a manner despite the cries that rent the air around it seemed obscene. Yet it did. I came closer to it, carefully picking my way through the rocks and trees so as not to be detected.

All around the fire was chaos.

I saw many men, some of them looking for all the world

like men who would have sat in the saloon. White men with beards and guns at their belts and heavy boots. Several of them were on horses, and it was clear that it was not their camp. The other men had a yellow pallor to their skin and heads with no hair except for long braids that started near the crown of their skulls and fell all the way down their backs. They wore what looked like robes over loose pants, some blue and some white. It was these latter men who were emitting the screams of terror.

Out to the left of the fire, one of the white men stood over the prone figure of one of the yellow men and hacked downwards with his blade. He tore a widening hole into the chest and stomach of the man. Odd shapes filled the hole and slithered in it, moving about as the blade chopped into them. Blood welled around the hole and poured over the man's sides onto the ground around him, making mud that sucked at the boots of the men who still stood.

As this happened in a manner so slow and profane, a bearded man chased down one of the men in blue garb. The bearded man, screaming, grabbed the long braid that trailed behind the other man and pulled him closer with it, twisting it around his clenched fist. I swore the braid would rip from the second man's head, but it held tightly to his scalp, exposing the throbbing veins of his neck. It was these exposed veins that the man with the beard severed.

The white men rode around the fire on their horses, their pistols flashing and exploding.

Beyond the fire, a man on his knees begged in a language completely strange to me, a tongue that rose above the way people generally talk. Wrapped in his robes, he looked like a holy man. He lifted two fine, long-fingered hands to the two men who stood before him. These men had guns drawn. They kicked the kneeling man with their heavy boots. One of them seized the thin wrist of the man on his knees and twisted it behind his back until he dropped down to the other hand. The second man stepped across the back of the man on the ground as if he were mounting a horse and fired his pistol into his skull.

The voice of the man on the ground fell silent. Perhaps only I could hear the absence of it in the symphony of screams it had once been a part of.

—That one's trying to run!

—Cut their goddamn pigtails off!

I turned and pressed my back against a tree wide enough to hide me from view.

The screams went on and on. When finally they died down, I heard a lone, high voice, calling out in that strange language. Then there was laughter and voices I could understand.

—This one's left. Fine face on it. Like a woman's.

It was some time before those screams of that final foreign tongue were silenced. When they were, they were replaced by the steady thrum of hoofbeats.

Only the Lord can say what they did to that last man. I hid in the darkness behind my closed eyes, my heaving back against the tree. What words could describe what happened around that campfire, the states all those men were brought to? My mind was blank—there was just a terrifying blackness.

I am not sure how to say what happened next. But I felt a rushing through me, like the wind had become a knife. I felt something cut through my body softly, all screams and tight tendons. I stood there, thinking perhaps what I had seen had driven my body to the brink of sickness or my mind to madness. But the feeling was gone as soon as it had come and did not recur.

For the longest time, I stood there in the trees. The sun fell some way in the sky. I waited for a sound, a return of the men. But nothing stirred. The fire, so silent before, crackled and burst behind me.

Finally, I turned towards the camp. In the much lessened light, I saw bodies lying all around the dying fire. Some barely resembled human forms, so defiled were they. The long braids had been chopped from most of their heads. As I walked among the carnage, as my boots slid across the bloody ground, I wondered what these men could have done to deserve this. Even in death they had been shown no mercy. Their bodies had been shown less consideration than slaughtered animals.

I have seen men die. But never have I seen death so savage.

I cannot push from my mind how much the rampaging men looked like the men from the saloon.

After I had grown numb to the horror, I went into the tents of the dead men and took what food I could find. May the Lord forgive me.

FEBRUARY 11, 1849

Wandering through the fog this last day, shaken and reeling, I stumbled upon a group of camps. At first, I could not be sure they were not the camps of the marauding men I saw yesterday, and I was hesitant to approach them. But soon, the men spoke of the massacre, and I realized they had not been a part of it.

I gleaned that the murdered men were Celestials who had been working in the mills nearby.

—Damn Chinamen make it so that no man natural born here can make a living, he said. —They work for nothing, so a man looking to make his fair wages can't nearly survive with them around.

The men used words and phrases like "invader" and "that manner of men" in such a way that made it clear they viewed those dead men as less than human. I could tell that they had not stood for even a second in the horror of the camp I saw yesterday.

—They took them Chinamen by surprise. One man laughed. —They never saw it coming.

Despite this surprise attack, I learned that one man from the victorious side of the battle had been killed. His body had been taken to a nearby camp and was to be buried this evening. The men I had come across were heading to his impromptu funeral. I could find no way of saying I would not accompany them.

The men dressed up in different clothes, just as they would to pay their respects in a world not as peculiar to them as this one. They tied ties around their necks and brushed the dust off their hats. Some of them combed beards that looked as if they had not been untangled in weeks. I felt strange watching them, my mind forever straying back to the brutal cries of those white men on their horses the day before. I felt strange, too, that I could only present myself as I stood, though I could not reckon that feeling with my discomfort to be paying any respects at all.

When we arrived at the other camp, I saw what might have been the angry faces I had seen yesterday. It was hard to tell, somber and clean and in mourning as the men were now. Their blue eyes rolled up, not infrequently, to the heavens. The guns that hung by their sides were polished. They winked peacefully in their holsters, as if they were there for nothing but show, to adorn the mourning clothes of these men. I heard expressions of grieving and condolence.

—He was a righteous man, and he died bravely.

—The Lord above will look fondly upon him.

—He has found his fortune in the life beyond.

The body, lying on a blanket near the hole in the ground, looked almost at peace. The men had not been able to hide

the wound that had killed him—it was plain that something sharp had been driven through his eye and into his
brains—but the blood from the wound had been washed
away, and his mouth and remaining eyelid had a look of rest
to them. His fellows had dressed him in his best clothes and
folded his hands across his chest. The lines of his shoulders
and his neck spoke of repose.

A man stepped up to the body. —In light of the fact
that there ain't no priest about, I've been chosen to say a few
words over the body. Jason here was a good man. He died
defendin' what is right, something he felt his duty as we
men travel here to the West, to this place sometimes seem-
ing forsaken by God and decency. It is the duty of righteous men like us to defend what we know to be true. To
make this land a place where we wouldn't be afraid to bring
our blessed women and our children. Jason died molding
and shaping a world that is so often savage and animal.
He leaves behind a beautiful woman out in the East, who
will be much saddened by the passing of her brave husband
but who has much to be proud of, too. Because of him this
Western world may someday become a place friendly and
familiar to the good and the God fearing.

The other men nodded solemnly. Some had tears in
their eyes.

—Amen.

It was then that I noticed the men had placed in their
dead friend's hand one of the long braids of the Celestials.
It twined between his folded hands like a rosary. Four men
gently lifted the blanket the dead man lay on and lowered

the body into the hole.

This was sundown. By the time all the light had slipped from the sky, the men I had met and I were back in their camp. They took off their ties and whatever else they had made themselves proper with, but an air of solemnity hung over the camp. I could find no joy in the light of the fire or the food they offered me. But our reasons were clearly of a different nature.

FEBRUARY 12, 1849

I again spent the day in the camp. The men are heading north in no great rush and are content for another day to play cards, sew clothes, and cook. Much as I want to find my wife in Coloma, I am loath to walk away from such a setting where food is, if not plentiful, available, and men welcome me. These men do not have the joy of the men I met two weeks ago nor do I trust them the way I trusted those first men. They are too close to the horror I witnessed. At times, as I study their faces, I cannot tell them apart from the marauders.

The men prospect halfheartedly for pay dirt as they make their way to the fields supposedly rich with it. They find some here and there but not enough, they say, to keep them. They dream of greater things.

There are four large tents in the camp, and each houses at least two men. One of the tents also houses all the cooking and food supplies. In front of another is a long plank across two big rocks that the men use as a card table. They play games learned from Mexicans, they say. It is a comfort to see the steady flashes of black and red that are playing cards; there is a rhythm to them that reminds me of the comforts I left behind.

Between two of the tents in the camp near the fire, they have strung a rope on which they hang their wet clothes. The clothes flit back and forth in the wind. At times the wind catches them, and they fly to their uppermost position on the rope, casting shadows over the ground. As we talk, the camp will shade dark, like a storm cloud has blown heavy and fast above us. Then the wind will whip the clothes back down, and the light will shine upon us, making our faces and hands and the white of our clothes glow bright in the new light.

Near the camp, there is a tree that I have frequently sat underneath the last two days. It has near-ebony bark, and its forest-green leaves grow close and thick in a halo around its upper branches. Deep maroon, nearly black, berries hang from these branches, and they are sweet when I crush them between my teeth. Their taste is pleasant to me, even with the food cooked over the campfire available. Small grey birds with some feathers even darker than the berries fly to and from the branches, pecking at the fruit and chattering amicably to one another. They share the branches with the occasional lightly colored moth or perhaps butterfly.

I am not a man unmoved by such beauty, and after the darkness of the last few days, such a sight has brought me great comfort. I have thought many times to write of this tree to Joanna and have even sat down to do so. But on that occasion, my pen's nib stopped before any words could flow onto the paper. I found it impossible to write her a letter of the beauty I saw knowing how much terror I would have to conceal.

Today after lunchtime had passed and I had washed the men's tin plates and bowls in the stream, I escaped the closeness of the camp to sit beneath the tree. I made myself comfortable in the dirt and idly traced my fingers over the dark bark. Its ridges and shallow valleys were entrancing to move my hands along, and I closed my eyes, enjoying the sense of touch alone. I moved my hand over the same patterns again and again, the same several square inches of bark. There, with my eyes closed, I imagined I had found an old, craggy face. The more I traced back and forth, the more it seemed to be there. Finally, I opened my eyes, half-expecting to see what I had imagined.

Instead, I saw Robert, one of the men from the camp, had joined me. He looked at me oddly, and I scrambled to explain. —Some tree bark, they say, can be used as medicine. Trying to break a piece of this one off.

Robert seemed to accept the explanation. He is a young man, much younger than me, and young men often let much go by as things they have not yet learned. The face in my mind was replaced by his. He has red hair, and his cheeks and chin are smooth. His eyes are a blue so dark that they are unsettling.

He asked to sit beside me and for some time wrote on a sheet of paper in longhand. I could not help but notice the evenness and flow of his writing. The nib of his pen scratched across the paper with a steady rhythm, as if he were composing poems and their meter was there in the sound of the pen.

After he had covered most of the front of the page, he looked up, his dark eyes focusing on me. —What do you know of the fields up north? he asked with an almost childlike reverence. —I'm writing my mother, and I'd like to know what you've heard. Being here so long, you must know lots of tales.

I thought of the setting described in Joanna's letters. —Just that there is gold being mined. And all that the mining of gold brings.

A dreamy look came over him, and I knew there was some distance between him and the campfire, the men playing cards, and even me who sat so close.

—I heard stories, he said, —that everywhere you scrape the ground, there's gold to be found. If you find a path through the trees, there's likely to be gold in every step. Men are making more in a day than they can make in a month back East. Men walk the streets of town heavy with gold in their hands and pockets. Gold can bring anything a man might want—the best food, a house with people serving you day and night, women if you want them, nice clothes, trips to the theatre, horses, cattle to raise. And it's all lyin' there for the taking. Most men don't even have to work very hard for it.

—Some of that sounds true, I said.

—Can you imagine, he said, looking up to a sky that could not match the blue of his eyes, —that gold was just lyin' there in the earth all this time? Doing nothing when it can do men so good? You wonder how many times men like you who've been living out here stepped right over it, thinking nothing of it. When all they had to do was take it, and the whole world would be theirs?

I agreed that it was hard to imagine.

—So rich, the land. And just a little digging, just a little tearing at it, and those riches are where they belong, with men who can do something with them, who can make a life and living out of them. Just by displacing a little bit of earth.

He made it sound so simple and harmless that I almost believed this subtle shift was all the men rushing west would do.

As he talked, his eyes against the sky unsettled me further. Perhaps I was still caught in the world of dreaming that he had interrupted. But I wondered again and again how those two shades of blue could exist together. It seemed his eyes or the sky must change. These odd thoughts plagued me nearly as much as the word "gold" falling out of every set of lips I encounter.

Later

This afternoon, I was standing at the fire when a cry rose from just beyond the camp. My blood froze in my veins, for it sounded like the cries of the massacring men two days ago. My spine went rigid, and my shoulders drew together, waiting for the attack to begin.

But instead of attacking men coming into the camp, all the men in the camp ran towards the screaming. The cries turned more articulate.

—Look at it shining there!

—It's beautiful!

—God bless this land of fortune!

The men had discovered something shining in the ground near the tree I sat under this morning. Some digging revealed the glint of all that was precious to them. I watched as the men crowded around the base of the tree. The birds that had gathered singing in the branches took flight, their dark undersides lifting to the sky, heading straight up, then away in a black cloud too dense to see beyond. Their shadows fell over the men, making their faces change for a moment into pits and shades. Then they were gone, not to return, I am sure.

The men dug frantically around the tree and found that a piece of gold the size of a man's head was tangled in the roots. They hacked at the roots with their shovels, but the formidable chunk of gold was like the heart of a man, all wrapped in the veins that were the roots of the tree.

The men did not notice as I walked back to camp and prepared my pack to leave. Last I heard of their argument, they had decided the best way to reach the gold and whatever pieces of gold it foretold was to chop down the tree and destroy its roots. I did not want to be there when their arguing turned to deciding which of the men that chunk of gold belonged.

FEBRUARY 13, 1849

Once again on my path, my mind turns to where I am heading or rather to whom I am heading. The more I focus on Joanna, the more I find refuge from all I have seen in her absence. It seems odd, I am sure, as what I have seen is part of the great world, and Joanna is but a woman, small, slight, and certainly no one to hide behind.

Yet I focus on the picture of her soft brown hair swept up from the back of her neck, and suddenly the image of the Celestial pulled by his braid as his throat was severed begins to blacken at the edges, to fade away. I think of her gentle smile, and the harsh shine of the Stranger's mouthful of gold teeth starts to recede in the same way. At present, I think of the soft curves of her breasts and her hips, and the sinewy figure of the Indian is replaced. To think of my sweet Joanna is like an amulet against all that is harsh, all that frightens or horrifies or befuddles me. A talisman.

The letter that took her to her family in Coloma came months ago. Her family has always been close, having traveled from Boston together by ship a short time before Joanna and I met. Her father was a merchant and had no plans of letting his youngest daughter be taken by the likes of me.

I can only too clearly remember how I used to make myself proper before her father. How harsh the light of the fire in the hearth of his home seemed as he sat against it, looking upon me and judging me. How soft that same light became as he allowed me a few moments with Joanna, how it fell upon the loose curls of her long hair and played in her gentle eyes. Those eyes so soft on me, so accepting, though I was hardly long out of the woods and the trees and the hunt, and it had been no time at all since I had made my living at the trading posts, pelts slung over my shoulders. Her father still saw that rough man beneath my facade of decency, heard the few trappers' phrases that still slipped around the edges of the higher language I used in front of him. But my Joanna had always seen something different.

When finally her father allowed me her hand, it was on the promise that I would never take her completely from the rest of them. That if ever there was a time of need, I would allow her to rejoin the family, to lighten the burden with her sweetness, her kind words, her gentle hands, her beauty so much like the light of a flame in a black night in this harsh frontier.

But by the time Joanna's father went into the farming business and moved north, I was already running the saloon, and it seemed that separated from the rest of her family she would be. Even then, even though I knew it would distance me from the light of her presence, the ease of her soft forgiveness, I told Joanna that I would never try to keep her from her family. There was only once she wished to be separated from me until the time the letter came.

Without Joanna, I tried to keep myself occupied. There was the saloon, and that provided me with much distraction. But still, often on the sleepless nights while she was gone, thoughts and memories I have never been able to reconcile began to creep at the edges of my mind. I become that lone man, hunting, taking life, making my own rules and ways—ones that the civilized world had no bearing on.

I think her name now to force those thoughts away. *Joanna, Joanna, Joanna.* The beginning of the word opens my lips silently, and the second half escapes them just as soundlessly in a soft push. I am glad there is no one to hear me talking to myself this way and think my mind touched. But her name, like a benediction of some sort, drives all else away. And for a moment, my mind is clear.

FEBRUARY 14, 1849

Today I found a feather lying in the dirt. It was a lone feather, and I almost stepped right over it without noticing it. As I turned to see what had caught my eye, something so white against the brown dirt, I saw it resting there, curling up at each end, telling me tales. Though it was in the dirt, it was not defiled by it. It shone as bright as if it had just fallen from a wing that flew high in the heavens. I picked it up.

I cannot be sure what happened next actually happened, for the sun was beginning to sink from the sky. But as I turned up the palm of the hand with the feather in it, I thought the lines etched in that palm ached a horrible red. The red I had seen in the Celestials' camp, where maroon blood mixed into the brown earth. I closed the hand over the white feather, my heart beating fast and my breath coming in short, quick gasps. I shut my eyes, and the blood pounded in the red blackness in my head.

I remembered another time, a time before Joanna's sweet calm and love had blessed my life. A time of musk, of the shadows of trees and wilderness falling black on me.

I saw myself crawling through the woods, approaching the place where a body had fallen with a dull thud to the ground, the life gone from it. And me stalking and crawling, me coming through the bushes, parting them. And the blood on my hands. The blood on my hands.

Lost in the past, it was some moments before I could once again gaze at my hand and the feather. Both looked different. The lines of my palm were the same color again as the rest of my flesh, mere shallow ravines set in the slightest of shadow. The feather was no longer shining white but dusted with the dirt of the path. I stared at both in the failing light, searching them and imprinting them in my memory lest they change once more. But the feather was just a fallen feather, and my hand was my own.

FEBRUARY 15, 1849

The fog returned, swirling and crowding thick about me. I walked down its corridors, and my thoughts went down the twisting pathways of my mind. For every step I took in the misty world, I moved forward to some trail of memories until I found myself lost on the path my feet walked and also the one inside my mind. Sharp recollections reared up. I saw them almost as clearly as if they were images forming in the dense fog around me.

I recalled this one time I saw two men kill each other. It was in the general store in this little town that only recently had been nothing more than an outpost. One man was behind the counter, holding bread. And this other man who looked as though he had seen hard times was trying to get that bread, but he didn't have enough money. I suppose the man behind the counter thought he was protected by something, maybe what he thought of as rights and owning. He held that bread away, and by God he looked surprised when the other man lunged at him, grabbing it. They started to tear at each other. The bread fell away, and there was just those two men ripping and clawing at one another. And bleeding from their faces and losing eyes and beating one another's heads off the ground. The man from behind the counter finally got a shot off that ripped apart the other man's face. But he fell to the floor and didn't get up, either. And there was that bread, all covered in their blood and brains.

And then right on the heels of that recollection came this other one. I was doing business with a man in his house, and outside it was raining hard and heavy. We heard this noise like a woman's scream. And we stepped outside into the rain, and in the fields his mare was standing with her muscles tight and her mouth open. She was straining and screaming, and the man told me she was close to birthing, but he did not know this close. Her body shuddered, and the foal dropped from her and hit the ground like a sack of rocks. Born dead. The mare, she stopped screaming and walked away, as if she knew better than to bother. And that body was lying there in the rain, and there was just this smooth flatness where its face ought to have been.

And I barely registered that monstrosity, that lacking, when another memory came hard and fast. A man in my saloon, sitting near me at the bar and not saying anything for the longest time, just looking around from beneath bushy eyebrows with eyes I didn't trust. Dark eyes against his light skin. Eyes that were burning hot—simmering is more like it. Like he'd pushed their fire down for the sake of hiding it.

He got to drinking, and those eyes got to burning again, and he got to talking. His words were slower than even the drink should have made them, strained and sliding slowly as if he were enjoying them so much that he didn't want their taste leaving his mouth. He told me in great detail about a squaw he had killed. How he had first blown the head off her baby as she held it. Then he had beaten her with his gun. Then finally he shot her. Here he laughed slow and deep and told me the part he had been saving—each time he'd shot his gun, he'd held it in front of his crotch *so that bitch and her baby had the taste of my cock on them when they went out of this world.*

I reeled in the fog, these pictures and words crowding in my mind. They piled up and pressed about one another, so I could not force them out. I tried to think past the end of each one. And each time, I arrived at the same thing: walking into the house and those stories spilling out. Telling the horrors to Joanna as the numb terror froze me. And there she was listening. Taking my words quietly as if she would bear them for me. There she was lifting those smooth, white hands to my temples, rubbing them, easing my strain. And always there was this peace flowing from her soft hands into me.

I stumbled through the fog, picturing a candle.

And then the fog began to clear. The feathers were all around me like fallen leaves. I found them on the ground, caught in plants like white flowers, hanging from trees like blossoms. I felt something soft catch against my cheek and reached up to find that a feather had blown in the wind from my left and rested there. The wind pulled it from my fingers, passed it against my wet lips, where it paused for another moment, then took it.

My boots carried me down through some rocks into

a small ravine of sorts. The rocks stood about fifteen feet above my head, and the ones on the ground were slick with moss. I stumbled over them, at times thinking my journey would end with my head dashed on them. The more I walked, the more I gained my footing. I felt less like the rocks were a danger and more as if they were a shelter. A peaceful feeling settled over me when I had steadied myself enough to hear the rocks echoing my breath all around me. The feathers fell out of the sky like the petals of blossoms whose time has passed.

I found the Indian sitting on a rock, doing what I supposed was cursing in a language I couldn't understand. His head was in his hands, and his long hair twisted down to the rock beneath him. His voice rose but in the way the beat of a hammer rises, steady and deep yet somehow filling the air so much it can only lift into the sky.

I stood there watching him, feeling as if my observing was perverse. I shifted my now-firm footing a bit before clearing my throat. —Hello?

His head snapped up. His eyes were sharp on me, but I could see that the rest of his face had gotten worse, fallen further into whatever disintegrating sickness had hold of him. The bumps had begun to build upon each other, looking more like mounds of redness. His eyes softened from their hard, piercing state as he seemed to recognize me. — That damn Coyote. These damn feathers.

The feathers were still falling. Some of them landed in his hair, and for a moment I thought they were weaving themselves back in the mess there. Perhaps they were. There is so little I can say with certainty.

With a final whisper, the last of the feathers seemed to fall. There was a silence around us as gentle as our breathing had been. It was as if the feathers that were now scattered on the ground were softening our surroundings, making it silent and holy. But can one call anything "holy" in a world like this? I thought "holy" next to the memory of what I had seen just a few days prior, and a terror at the juxtaposition nipped at the back of my mind. I suppose it showed on my face.

—You are not the man I left behind, are you? the Indian asked me.

I began to answer him, but I stopped myself. —I am no longer sure.

He nodded once in a manner that told me he expected my answer or at the least was not surprised by it. —You have seen much in a short time, haven't you?

I was quiet for a moment. I clutched the straps of my pack, which dug deep into my hand. —I have seen more than I ever wished to.

Again, he favored my words with his single dispassionate nod. He waited. Now that the feathers had stopped falling he seemed content to stare at me in silence.

—Men, I said finally. —Men of kinds I have never seen. Speaking words I have never heard spoken. But they are not the ones who bother me. It is the men who look familiar and talk like I do. Those are the men who have made me wonder why the earth hasn't gotten rid of all men in some way so they will never return.

A smile without mirth or enjoyment distorted the Indian's lips. —It is not many white men who can see the other white men for the graceless beasts they are.

I told him the story of the camp of Celestials. Images came through my words that I had not allowed into my consciousness. How the guts of one of the Celestials were white and yellow, despite all the blood, and how they had still seemed to pulse and squirm like earthworms, even though the body had taken on the stillness of death. The strange, smooth stones on a board that I had found in a tent that was either a game or a divination method, a mystery I would never know the answer to. The vegetables roasting on the fire that had been splattered in the blood and gore of their dead bodies, taking on an aroma of human meat cooking.

The words poured out of me in torrents, emptying from my mouth as a waterfall rushes over rocks. They went on and on, and I recoiled from them. When I finally stopped, I realized that not only words had been coming from me but also tears and mucus, which wet my face and made it slick.

The Indian watched this display in stoic silence. He fingered the buckskin bag at his side that I knew to hold the gold he wanted so much to be rid of.

I wiped my face with the sleeve of my shirt. The Indian and I regarded each other from our places in the ravine. The silence was different now, wet and heavy, like the silence after rain.

—These men looked like you, he said.

—They could have been my brothers.

It must have been the weakness brought on by the

memories of the slaughter, but another memory, one I do my best to keep at bay, came to me of the first time Joanna went away. When I was a younger man, I was not insusceptible to the temptations of whisky, and once I had drunk far too much of it. That night, I entered the house I shared with Joanna, and some little daily action of hers sent me into a fit. I screamed at her, and she cowered from me in a corner.

When the whisky's spell took its leave of me, I felt great guilt and apologized to my wife in a tearful manner. She forgave me but described for my edification the rage that had marred my face as I shouted at her. She spoke in detail of the lines and shadows of my face, the snarl of my lips, the lowered brows and the lined forehead, the fury in my eyes. She said it would be best to not see me for a time until the memory could fade. She sent for her brother to accompany her north and made herself almost invisible to me until he arrived.

As I stood in the ravine, Joanna's words returned to me, and I knew even more that my face resembled the faces of the men I had seen, more so than I ever wanted to believe.

The Indian continued to study my countenance as if it held signs of what would come to pass. —It will be difficult for you, if you ever want to wear a different face.

—But I am not like them, I insisted. —Those men . . . what they did . . . I have never . . . I could never . . .

—Ever remains to be seen.

Perhaps it was the emotions I felt from telling the story, but I did not have the strength to correct him any further.

The Indian continued to sit there on his rock. As he did so, he reached into the leather pouch he kept at his side. As his fingers dallied there, I could hear the soft metal sounds of the pieces of gold touching one another. The sounds were almost musical. They traveled to the walls of the ravine and did not bounce back, like other sounds did, but seemed to be absorbed by the rock, tucked away there safely.

The Indian lifted his hand from the pouch, holding a piece of gold the size of a button. He looked down at it, smiling that same joyless smile. Small as the smile was, it seemed to twist the mess of his face painfully.

The Indian gracefully opened the thumb and the finger that were pinched around the gold, as if he were releasing some spot of magic dust into the air. The gold dropped straight down to the ground. The earth seemed to stir in a barely perceptible way, like the stirrings of a burrowing insect under the skin of an animal. Less and less of the shining rock was visible in the seconds that passed until finally its shine disappeared altogether.

The Indian's eyes met mine, and they seemed to find a sliver of peace. The half smile seemed less strained. But it lasted only a moment. I felt the slightest tremble beneath my boots, as if the ground had hiccupped, but it was enough to remove the smile, however joyless it might have been, from the Indian's face. He lifted his chin and set his mouth in a hard line. He appeared to be bracing himself.

Directly under the Indian's hand, which was still raised in the air like a graceful bird frozen in flight, a crack appeared in the ground. It was not wide but seemed quite deep. Other cracks began to run from it like a spiderweb. Then the initial crack widened. In the center appeared a hole.

Like a slug pulling itself out of the earth, the piece of gold reappeared. It crept up and up as if propelled by legs or a cinching motion that I could not see at work. It appeared bigger than before, and as it rose I could see that it was. Like the earth had been gestating something new from a seed.

The Indian touched his forehead, which had sunk below his shoulders. He held his hand there as if it were a thing of great heft but little value. He muttered words I could not understand.

—If I were a white man, he said in English, —I would think myself richer now.

The cracks in the earth stopped forming but did not mend themselves. The piece of gold sat in them like a stone set in a ring. The Indian picked it up. —Not here, he said. —We must travel.

Our footsteps echoed through the ravine. The fallen feathers had ceased to muffle the sounds of the world.

FEBRUARY 16, 1849

We travel by day now that I know the Stranger is traveling by night. We made our camp this evening, and in the light of the fire by which I write, the Indian told me this story:

—There was a battle in which my people suffered a fate like the men you saw. Months ago, before I began my journey, before I worked for the white man who pretended to own the land where the gold was first found, there was a group of white men who camped in the north. They wore the most ridiculous clothes, as if they had come to these lands expecting their life to be some fandango day and night. Silly hats that stood tall from their heads and big black bows around their necks and fine suits and shoes. Mixed in with them were a few brown men dressed just as ridiculously. They had horses that they kept poorly. The animals suffered at their hands as if they were worthless possessions, not things with life of their own. They beat them needlessly and never worried themselves about the condition of the beasts' hooves or mouths.

—One day the horses were gone. Perhaps some of my

people stole them and ate them, as those men who had the horses had already killed many of the things we would have chosen first to eat. Or perhaps the men were drunk and miserable and forgot to secure them. That is not important. What is important is that the horses were gone, as if they had never been there.

—These white men blamed my people who were near them. They thought all my people savages and thieves who could never respect the property of men in a way that is proper. And maybe they were right about property, that we could not find respect for the things they claimed to own. We heard the first stories about their horses and their anger, and we knew there would be a war. We have seen wars before. So we waited.

—It was during a ceremony of ours when they came. It is a ceremony that I am not sure I can make a man like you understand. Something that avenges the dead. There were many dead among us by then, and we knew at the hands of who—men who were paid good money for the bloody work of severing our heads from our bodies. Still others had been led away in chains to places only the Spirit knows. Many more of our children had been stolen, taken as slaves. The white men's fences kept us from our plants and medicine and our swamps. White men beat us and lynched us and tortured us. So, to speak to these injustices, there was a statue of a man who looked something like you, and we threw rocks at it, cut it with our knives, and beat it with our fists. And we invited these men who had owned the horses, these men who also resembled the statue, to come look upon the effigy they matched. That is our custom.

—Besides that statue and those men, my cousins were there. My mother with her bone necklaces. And my sisters, still so young they wore nothing, were free to roam with the nakedness of youth, as is also our custom.

—But as we tore at the statue as a symbol, they tore at us in a way that was no symbol.

—I heard a gunshot from between the trees. The men had approached without a sound. Friends, I suppose, of the men we had invited to the ceremony. After I heard the shot, I saw the face of one of my relatives explode like a piece of ripe fruit thrown against the bark of a tree. It was there in all its fineness and delicateness, then it was a pulp of redness without shape. My relative fell to the earth.

—The friends of the men we had invited to the ceremony appeared through the trees, their faces painted even whiter. Perhaps they were mocking the way some Indians paint their faces for battle, or perhaps it was a trick of their deviousness, the way Kah'-kool painted himself black to blend into the night. Their faces were unnatural, like demon spirits. They hung in the darkness, moved like ghosts between the trees, with the features twisted and long and pointing in the wrong directions. They wove in and out of the white branches, mixing with them and looking as if they came out of them.

—We fought them. I killed one myself, feeling his blood spill around my knife as I cut into him. I had never killed a man before, and in that moment, I felt all his life rush out at me. But it was not long before one of his fellows tried to avenge him. Bullets hit the ground around me as he shot wildly in my direction. One hit my leg, and the pain was great. I suppose he had no more bullets, for when he came close, he hit me across the face with his gun. I felt the brokenness there as I fell to the ground. I must have appeared dead because he did not continue his attack but moved on to others.

—I could do nothing but float in and out of this world as the battle raged on around me. I heard screams and felt the spirits of my people and the white men brush by me in the darkness. Many of the spirits were dead, and I knew that I must not have been dead because they recoiled at my smell. One spirit grabbed my hand and pulled me along a path lined with black roses. The roses grew, the heart of their petals moving, as if there were swarms of beetles inside them. But then I yanked my hand away and drifted back to the world.

—I heard a man speaking near me. *Cut their savage scalps off*, he said. Another man asked what they would do with them. *Keep them as souvenirs*, the first said. *Send them back home to show the triumph of decent men over savages. Dry them out, and keep them in a box to hold in old age. Put a piece of them on a necklace.* A third man laughed and said, *Make a wig from them for when you go bald.* Then someone said, *Sell them, you idiot.* Of course that is what they would do. The prices for pieces of my people were high. I heard the sound of their knives on skin.

—Again, I was on the midnight path with black flowers. The path crossed over a narrow bridge, and I tiptoed across it. I slipped and fell and fell, falling like in a dream where there is no bottom to the ground you slip on, just the dark chasm of unknowing. After what seemed like days, I hit the earth where I lay without moving.

—When I awoke, the men were gone. I was lying next to the body of one of my people. My arms had been wrapped around him and my lips pressed against his. I disentangled myself from his rigid embrace, and pain shot through my head and leg. I raised my torso, my arms planted into the ground. All around me, the bodies of my people had been placed in positions as if they were making love to each other. My mother and my sisters and my cousins as well. Their bodies were rigid and lifeless, some without heads, some without arms or legs, some without scalps. My mother's long, beautiful black hair had all been cut away. The white men seemed to have had quite a time coming up with the positions they left us in. Not a body was left out of them. The bodies of their own, they had taken away.

Here the Indian lowered his head. —I wished to disentangle them, to show their bodies some sort of respect. To not leave them rotting like animals in the sun. To not leave them in these positions. But my pain was too great, and it was all I could do to drag myself through the trees, back to people who could help me. So I left them there like that. I pray that their bones are not still in those positions in which the white men left them.

—I was sick for a long time after. The metal of the white man's bullet has still not left me, and at times I believe it sings out. Many times, in the fever that burned through my body in the coming weeks, I looked again for that midnight path I had found the day of the battle. This time, I swore to myself, I would not fall from it. I would hold the black roses in my teeth until their motion became part of my mind, until I found peace in them. But I could never find it again. My mind wandered many ways, but I had lost that path. It seemed lost for good.

Around us the night surged with the blue black of twilight and the sounds of the winged insects that flew against the shaded skies. I wanted to say something that would distance me from the men in his story. But there we sat in silence.

—I can still taste where the blood on my face mingled with the blood on the face I awoke pressed against. Nothing in the stories of my people—not the story of Yel'-lo-kin or His'-sik, the thunder, the river mermaids, the underworld people, or even the story of the beginnings of death—could have prepared me for that.

My dear,

I wish I had words to write you that could bring you some light or joy, but those are not the ones you will find here.

Stephen has been gone nigh a month, and no one has heard from him. A body of a young man was found recently a few days' travel north of here, and Father is leaving today to see if the lifeless form belongs to his beloved son.

The possibility has greatly shaken Mary and me. They say the body was riddled with bullets and bespeaks a terrible end. Mary and I have spoken quietly, so that Father could not hear, of how Stephen may well have come across someone intolerant of his quick temper and tendency towards anger. Yet we pray for his safety.

Naturally, the news has been kept from Mother. Yet she seems to have intuited that something is wrong. She has not spoken in days, and sometimes we find her weeping softly in her bed. We beg her to tell us what troubles her, but she only shakes her head as the tears continue to fall. They are like silent rivers that flow without end. Even in the night, as we watch her sleep, they leak from her closed eyes, wetting her pillow. We fear that if it does not stop, she will lose all the moisture from her body.

The bad feelings in the house have become palpable. Little Josephine cries often for no reason, as if a bad spirit brushed by her little body. After perhaps her fifth fit of tears this morning, Mary and I took her out of the house to breathe fresh air. Josephine ran and played outside for some moments, then, with a

sigh, lay on her back on the ground. Mary and I looked to one
another, smiling, and crouched near her. The baby smiled at
us, pleased we had joined her.

We stayed there for a few minutes before Mary pointed to
the sky. White clouds hung there like cotton, startling against
the blue.

—Look, darling, she said to Josephine. —It is a cow in
the sky.

I stared at the cloud, and, lo, it did begin to look like a cow
with a lowered head, a wisp of a tail, and a clump of white for
its dull, benign face.

The baby must have seen it as well, for she giggled. —Mama!
she cried, laughing in a way she has not in days. —Again!

As if times were less troubled, Mary and I gestured to
shapes in the sky, creating images from them. A string of pearls,
a dinner knife, a coin, a man's boot, a bow, a bottle, a leaf. The
baby's joy inspired us, and we went on and on, stretching our
imaginations.

The clouds moved slowly in the sky, an ever-shifting canvas. The breeze was warm and bright. I could smell the earth
around us. All was simple joy. I tilted my head back, searching
for more shapes. It was then that I froze.

My dear, what has become of my mind? It is filled always
with horror. I see it even in a simple game.

In the sky, I thought I saw the head of a man. There were
spots of blue sky for the two eyes, and a long cloudless strip
was his mouth. The mouth was twisted gruesomely. The head
was attached to nothing, and I imagined it detached by some

horrible force. As the winds shifted, the face seemed to contort in a silent scream.

I gasped. As absorbed as they were in play, neither Mary nor Josephine heard my soft exclamation. I closed my eyes tightly. When I reopened them, the wind had shifted the face into something shapeless. The simple white cotton of a formless cloud. Next to me, the game went on. But I remained frozen, waiting to find some other horror in the sky. The blood in my veins seemed cold and did not warm me as it moved.

I rose, saying I needed to check on Mother. It suddenly seemed that the dark interior of the house, which holds so much sickness and sadness, was easier to bear than the horrifying sky and the images that played across it.

My dear, there is no comfort to be found here. Your letters have ceased, and I beg you now to pick up your pen, to write to me of your life, your days, the life that awaits my return. Write to me of the clothes that hang in our closets, of the sun that slants through our window at sundown. Bring me, for a moment, to a world beyond the one I live in daily. A world safe from this one. I must know that such a world still exists.

I await your words.

With all my love,
Joanna

FEBRUARY 17, 1849

I think back to the days when Joanna and I were first married. The way she did things—laying out clothes for the next day before she went to bed, lining up trinkets she valued along shelves, brewing such strong coffee in the morning that its scent woke me as much as the sunlight did, singing bits of songs as she made her way about. And over the years, her ways became my ways, so that our lives were like two rivers that had winked at each other through a distance in the trees until they started running together.

And when she was gone—that one time my actions drove her away and again just before my journey began—there was an absence. A quietness and an emptiness. There were still her things lined up on the shelves, and I still laid my clothes out the way she had, but there was too much space when I breathed. Too much room in my bed. Chairs were empty in ways they were not when she was simply out walking. I clattered about our rooms like the last of something in a tin, loud and small. Banging and clanking. All around me nothing but space.

There came a longing, too. A wish for things to be right and as they were. Somehow, though I never claimed to know much about what right and wrong is, I knew that Joanna was firmly in the camp of right. Therefore, to be away from her must be wrong. And in that absence of right, all I could wish for was her.

These thoughts go through my mind. This journey, this making my way towards her, must be right. What else can it be?

FEBRUARY 18, 1849

The Indian left our camp before I awoke this morning. There was not a trace of him left behind, not even the smallest of feathers. I know I will not see him again until fate winds our paths together once more. But can the word "fate" be used in this dark and terrifying world? A notion of rightness and design, a pattern that will someday make sense? Fate. I struggle with the notion. Then I think of how, sometime years ago, Joanna's family got on a boat and left the place where they were comfortable and safe and moved out here to this emptiness and wildness, and in all this empty space, she found the spot where I was standing. And I think how many words had to be spoken, how many steps had to be taken to put my wife's hand into mine. Suddenly I believe in things I have no right to. Things contrary to everything I see—the men fighting and killing and ripping up the land and losing their sense of value. Fate isn't something that makes sense. But how do you explain things like Joanna finding me? Or the Indian finding me? I don't see any way to do it.

These thoughts rattled in my mind. Alone, I wandered again, directionless. My legs, which are unaccustomed to the walking I have been doing, began to tire. My pack hung heavy on my back. My gun felt like a weight at my side. My shoulders sloped downward, all the burden of this journey hanging on them. My feet shuffled through the moss and brush on the ground, catching and stumbling.

It was past midday when I emerged from the trees into a wide field. Far away, I could see where the trees began again and where the mountains crouched. But the field was long, sparsely populated with low yellow flowers that fluttered in the light breeze. Once, I would have called these flowers "golden," but no longer can I do so. I walked out into the field.

I was perhaps a hundred yards into it when the tiredness overcame me completely. I lowered myself to the ground. The nights have grown cooler, and the earth, even in the sun as it was then, retained some of that coolness. I rested my back flat on it, feeling the damp ground beneath me while the warmth of the sun beat down onto my face and stomach and hands. This sun I once, too, would have referred to as "golden."

I opened my eyes to the dome of the sky. The blue seemed to stretch and stretch. I loosened the buttons of my shirt to feel the sun upon the skin of my chest.

At first, images, the words of the Indian, the troubles of my travels, the days that stretched behind and the ones that stretched ahead filled my mind. They paraded through it like men on horseback thrumming across an open field.

Then, just as the sound of hoofbeats recedes as they pass, the thoughts seemed to travel to the edges of my mind and disappear along its horizon. I felt something like peace.

In the blankness that my mind became, a wish sprang up like water bubbling from the ground. I wished not only that my journey was over but that all my journeys were over. That I could lay here at rest, leaving behind this world and its changes. That I could sink into the ground, feel it pull at me the way river mud pulls at my boots as I cast a fishing line over the water. The wish was so strong that all motion seemed to leave my body, even the pulsing of my own heart and the blood it drew through me. I started to fade into this wish, to drift away upon it.

I must have slept, for when I opened my eyes, the sun was gone and my body was shot through with cold. I fastened my shirt and tugged it close around me. I stood up. There was not much light to see by save that of a half-full moon. But I swore I saw a ridge around the place where my body had lain, as if the dirt had lapped around me like water, rising against my sides where it met resistance. The indentation was shallow but in my shape.

In the night, I walked on.

FEBRUARY 20, 1849

Today at dusk, I came upon a town. Perhaps "town" is too grand a word for it, as it is really a small collection of houses and stores, all of them made of grey wood and a few stones and weathered by many harsh years. People wandered the streets, men who do not have the look of a new journey on them, men who look as if the roads they travel now are the same roads their feet have walked upon for some time. It seemed a place yet untouched by the mining fever. I found that hard to believe, and, as it turned out, my lack of belief was well founded.

I was happy as I walked the streets, for I saw a store where new provisions would be available to me. Again, after the departure of the Indian, I have been reduced to eating that which I can find growing. Several times I have seen small animals scamper across my path and was tempted to use my gun on them, yet there is the vow I made so long ago, before Joanna came along, to take no more life, as insignificant as that life may seem. It is a vow I stand by even as my hunger gnaws at me.

As I made my way through the winding dirt roads, I felt the narrow passageways opening up a small measure at a time. I was not wrong in my feeling, for before I knew it I was standing in a square. It was only big enough for perhaps two wagons to enter at once. The space held no wagons, but still it was not empty.

Working in the center square were many men. Tools in hand, they toiled around piles of wood and marble. Set around these yet formless piles of material were the finished products of their labor. At first, I thought they were boxes and statues. But as I came closer, the boxes took on their true shapes, and the statues revealed themselves for what they were. The square was filled with coffins and head-stones. With the preparations for death.

I stood against a grey building, staring. I had never seen so many coffins stacked upon one another. The gravestones were lined up in rows, standing as they would someday over graves. At the ends of the rows, I could see incomplete etchings: *Sacred to the Memory of . . . , Final Resting Place of . . . , Who Practices God's Will in Death as in Life . . . , Here Lies . . . , Beloved . . .*

There were others full of carvings rather than words. One had the image of a small cherub. Another was covered in weaving vines that blossomed into elaborate flowers near the corners of the stone. There were large and small ones. I thought the small ones were for children, but there are so few children in these parts. They must have been for those who didn't have enough money to be buried under one of the elaborate stones.

In a haphazard pile near the small stones lay some

wooden crosses. They were, I suppose, for those who could not afford even a small stone. I thought of how some markers would last forever, and some would rot away within a few seasons. It didn't seem right that even death could be decorated with such favors and disgraces. But there it was.

A man looked me up and down, squinting, almost as if he was trying to see into me, to see what kind of man lay behind my skin. His eyebrows lowered, and he spit brown juice on the ground; maybe he did not like what he saw.

I turned away, unwilling to have any conflict with him. I looked towards the buildings that surrounded me, their dark windows and the dark shapes that moved inside them. When I looked back, the man was hammering at the wooden coffins, pulling at them now and then to make sure they were sturdy.

I gazed across the square and noticed a building with a sign that proclaimed it to be an inn. The thought of a bed after many hard nights on the ground with only my blanket around me was so appealing that I headed towards it right away. Though the straightest direction would have been through the square, I could not bring myself to walk through the piles of coffins and gravestones. I walked around the edge of the square, leaving a gap between me and the men working the wood and marble.

As I opened the door to the inn, I heard a soft tinkling above it and saw that the door's arc was in the path of a few strings of shells that brushed together when the door hit them. It was the only piece of decoration. In the little room were a heavy oak stairway and a doorway beyond which looked to be a dining room with a single long table in it. There was a desk opposite the stairs, and behind it sat a man. He was clean shaven, and his dark hair was cut neatly. Despite his fastidious appearance, he did not look like an easy man. His face seemed set around a scowl that may well have been a permanent feature. His jaws slowly worked a piece of tobacco that bulged out his left cheek.

—What can I help you with? He spoke like I was an inconvenience standing there.

—I'm looking for a room for the night or maybe the next two, I said.

He nodded, the scowl not leaving his countenance. — Rooms we have plenty of.

We settled on a price for the night. He took my money as if it were a favor to me. Then he led me up the creaking walnut stairs to the room.

It was a bleak affair, just a bed with an old oak headboard that shivered and quaked as I set my pack down on the mattress. There was a square of a window, but as the room faced the east, it caught none of the day's fading light. Only the shadows hanging from the roofs and the branches of the trees entered there.

—Last meal of the day is in an hour. Piss pot's under the bed.

I thanked him as he left the room.

I looked out over the square. The men had lit lanterns and were still toiling away at their grim trade. Hammers and chisels sounded dull clinks in the growing blackness. The shadows cast by the lanterns made the faces of the marble cherubs sinister, more darkness than light and fineness. The shadows caught the whole head of one of the stone angels, and it looked as if it had been decapitated. As I watched the men, the words "work" and "toil" didn't seem enough. What they had set upon was something endless. Something that went into the night, beyond their own hammers swinging, making nonsense of time.

I observed these men for a stretch before I heard a bell sound from inside the inn. I walked away from the window and down the stairs to the dining room. Four men sat at the long common table. The man from behind the desk who had shown me my room served plates of food to them, then moved behind a low, mahogany bar that was badly scratched. There he stood with his arms across his chest, not moving but for blinks of his eyes. He seemed to be waiting.

I sat at a spot set with a fork and knife and a plate of steaming food. On it, there were gristly chunks of meat in a brown, oily sauce and a green vegetable that had been cooked until it didn't resemble much of anything. I began to eat it as if it were a delicious feast. I was mopping up the gravy with a piece of bread when the man sitting next to me spoke.

—Where you traveling to? he asked.

I looked up. He was an older man with deep lines creased around his mouth and his eyes. He had the unkempt appearance of a man who has known no steady home in some time. —North. I intend only to stop in this town for a bit. Lured by a decent bed and some warm food, I suppose.

—You ever seen a town like this? He did not wait for an answer before adding, —I ain't never seen a town like this. Try to sleep at night, but those men in the square keep up their bangin' and chiselin' to beat the band. All hours. Why, I build coffins in my dreams.

—They work their trade all hours? I asked.

—Oh yes. It never properly stops.

—Why do you suppose that is?

—I don't rightly know, the man said. He reached out to a hat that sat next to his plate and fondled the dome as if it were the head of a child he was quite fond of.

—The trade's booming.

I turned to where the voice had come from and was surprised to see that the innkeeper had been moved to speak.

The other men at the table stopped eating to look at the innkeeper. They seemed as surprised by the occasion of his words as I was.

—Day and night, they work, and still they can't keep up with the need. So many men coming from all over, coming and living and dying, their legs rotting in the water they stand in all day, their bodies getting sores they can't cure, picking up diseases they was never prepared to fight. Used to be that we had a small trade in this town, building a coffin here, carving a stone there, someone from another town picking up the few things we'd made. Death used to be sparse and natural, the end of a life. It was an occasion. Now it's comin' in a flood. Comin' by boats and wagons and on horseback. Droves of men dying. So that we kept addin' men to work the trade, teachin' sons, bringin' men from other towns. Death is so common we don't even bother callin' it an event no more. A Mexican dance has more fanfare to it. Some days it seems like there's people arrivin' for no other purpose than to up and die. To lay their heads down on the new frontier. And we can't but accommodate them. The men of this town been makin' money hand over fist dealin' in stones and boxes. Like I says, the trade's booming. No time to stop for nothing.

Then the innkeeper looked away from us. He took a knife from his pocket, opened it, and pared at his fingernails. Outside the inn, the sounds of hammers and chisels were muffled by the walls.

Time passed, and the men around me sat, their digestive juices working at the meals in their stomachs. The innkeeper continued paring his nails, and I mopped my plate with my last piece of bread, pushing it around the circle of stoneware until it was as clean as if licked by a hungry dog. In the silence, the innkeeper splayed his hand out across the scarred bar and jabbed the knife into the wood between his fingers. The steady thock, thock of the knife finding wood built in speed, drowning out the sounds coming in from the square. He ran the knife back and forth, back and forth, not stopping and not even looking down.

—Didja ever hit? the man who had spoken to me asked him.

The innkeeper stuck the knife into the wood, then raised his hand to us. The top of his middle finger was missing. —Oh yes.

—And ya keep playin' at it anyway, the man said.

The innkeeper resumed the steady back and forth of the knife point between his fingers. —Man's got to pass the time somehow.

FEBRUARY 21, 1849

Resting my bones in the bed last night, surrounded by the four walls, was such a pleasure that I decided to stay here another day. The innkeeper seemed neither happy nor unhappy to have the business. I spent the morning trying to write Joanna, but nothing came of it. I gave up when the lunch bell rang at noon.

After lunch, I went to the front of the inn where the man I had spoken to yesterday watched the square. The workers had not stopped completely but took lunch in shifts. Near them at the edges of the square, two Mexican women stood with giant steaming pots. There was a wagon selling fruit, too, but most of the fruit seemed bruised or rotted. The men on break had plates out and lined up to buy beans and tortillas from the Mexican women, ignoring the fruit wagon. The women stoically took the money from the men and ladled the beans, not smiling and only speaking to one another occasionally in rushed Spanish. They stared down at the beans and tortillas, betraying nothing of what they were thinking.

The man who was staying at the inn with me spat tobacco juice onto the ground. It bubbled in the dirt. —You ever have a woman like that?

—No, I answered. Already the conversation was giving me discomfort.

—They ain't like our women, you know, he said with smug knowledge. —They get themselves in heat and need a man to cure it for them. Like the way a bitch does. I been waiting days, watching them women to see if they have the need. I can tell by lookin' at 'em. Their eyes get wild, and they're all smiles for you, rubbin' up against you every chance they get. But I guess it ain't their time. Which is a damn shame. I've had me all kinds of women, and I wouldn't say I liked that kind the best, but there sure ain't no harm in laying them when you get the chance to.

I rightly didn't know what to say, because I just stood there looking at the women. The woven reds, greens, and yellows of their long skirts made their eyes even darker. There was a distance, it seemed, between them and us. A space between our eyes and theirs. Their lives and our lives were like paths running alongside each other and refusing to meet. There would always be that distance, no matter how close they were.

—I heard tell a story about one of them Mexican women when I was traveling here from Texas. She was comin' up from Mexico with some men. Must not have been her time, or she wouldn't'a minded, but a man not with their party drug her off and had his way with her anyhow. Suppose you can't fault a man for needin' what he needs, but the story went that something of her ripped apart and tore loose. Not quite a woman no more, either piece of her, really. But that piece, that shadow piece that tore off, is out there roamin'. Mourning, this man said. And searchin', too, for the man that done it to her. Don't guess it'd be too particular to which man it found. Had a hard time sleepin' outside that night, thinkin' about it. Suppose it was just a story to pass the time, though.

—Men do tell stories to pass the time, I said. I do believe my hands were shaking a bit.

In the square, the men seemed to have fallen into a steady rhythm of hammer beats. Beat, pause, beat, pause, beat, pause. As I listened, the beats seemed more and more like drums. Then, off in the distance, I thought I heard cries. They were low, like rumblings from a faraway storm. They did not sound like the cries of men, were less full of deepness than that. I watched and watched to see what would come of them.

Before too long, some young boys rushed into the square. They grabbed at a few of the working men, who must have been their fathers. The boys looked excited. Their clothes were mussed up something terrible, and a few of their shirts and pants were stained. I tried to tell myself that the muddy red stains were not blood, but they looked just like it.

The men seemed chagrined to stop their work and indeed went on hammering despite the boys being there. The boys spewed out words and moved excitedly, trying to capture the older men's attention. Finally, some of the men put their hammers down.

Three larger boys appeared in the square. The oldest couldn't have been more than twelve years in this world. The boys dragged something smaller than them, though each of them had a hand on it. It looked like a brown sack with sticks splayed from it. As they came closer, I saw what could only be blood. These boys were covered in it.

Finally, the boys dropped the thing in a heap. It was a large fawn, not a newborn but nowhere near full grown. The larger boys danced over it.

One of them took a knife out of his pants and waved it in the air. It was covered in blood. —It tried to run, Pa! But we used our knives on it. We got it down on the ground, and we killed it!

The boys stabbed at the inert form of the fawn, demonstrating. The fawn did not have much of a face left by then.

One of the men laughed. —Well, I guess we have enough boxes to spare one for the animal.

—Boys hunting, the man next to him said, spitting casually onto the ground. —Does a man good to see.

All the men who had been buying beans and tortillas wandered away from the Mexican women. One of those women moved closer to the boys. She looked down at the dead animal, her face breaking its dispassionate countenance and showing the slightest look of disgust. She glanced at the bloody boys as she stepped back.

One of the older boys took notice of her, his eyes as hard as the man's who had stared me down the day before. He walked over to the fruit truck and bought two pieces of fruit. He threw them at the woman, one hitting her colorful skirt and exploding a red that might have looked bloody if not for the maroon blood so ready to compare it to on the boy's shirt.

The woman went back to where the beans and tortillas still sat steaming. Her face became expressionless once again. If the men noticed, they said nothing.

The boy returned to his friends, yelling with laughter.

The boys continued their bloody little dance in the square. I could not stand to watch more of it, though, and retreated to my room. I hovered over the piss pot, trying to hold down my vomit. Finally, the waves of nausea passed. It was not long after that I heard the hammers begin again. When I looked out the window, the body of the fawn had been dragged off to who knows where.

Later

The man who spoke to me of Mexican women outside the inn today was killed. It was dinnertime when a man at the opposite side of the table cleared his throat as if he had something caught in it. He cleared it again and again.

—You best stop that noise while I'm takin' food, the man who had spoken to me said.

The throat clearing stopped, but the man who had been doing it stared the other man down. He sneered, and I saw that his teeth were all but rotted from his skull. —Ain't no man going to talk to me that way.

The two other men at the table and I stepped back to a wall, away from where these two began swinging and cutting at each other. The man I'd been speaking to earlier pulled the other man's ear and sliced it clean away from his head. He transferred the ear from his hand to his mouth, held between his bared teeth, and there it stayed as the fight continued.

The table was overturned, its ornate iron legs standing straight up in the air. The man who'd been clearing his throat went behind the bar, sweeping bottles onto the floor as he grabbed for one that he turned, bell up, and swung at the other man. The reek of bad whisky and brandy flooded my nose.

The man who'd been clearing his throat broke the bottle over the face of the other man. His face seemed to break, too, dissolving into blood and gashes. The first man stabbed in lightning quick little jabs at the other man's face with the broken bottle neck. Finally, the neck found a home in the man's eyes. He stopped, stunned, as the man on the attack pushed the bottle neck in deeper with the heel of his hand. The man who had been stabbed fell to the floor, and the first man knelt over him, pushing and pushing the bottle neck as if he'd win a prize if he got it in there far enough. The other man's body flapped spasmodically a few times before lying still.

The man stood, wiping his hands on his pants. He glanced around the room, as if noticing us all for the first time. No one spoke. The murderer stepped over the body and towards the door.

None of us moved until long after we heard the front door of the inn open and close.

—Damn mess to clean, the innkeeper said. —They can

spare a box, but who the hell is left to clean this mess in here but me? Wish men would get to killing and dying somewhere else.

He ducked behind the bar and grabbed a broomstick that rested against the wall. He swept the floor behind the bar. The glass tinkled lightly, like the shells over the inn's front door just a moment before.

—Leastwise they both paid for the night, the innkeeper said.

I returned to my room and closed the door. Men die, I suppose. But tomorrow I am going to leave this town.

FEBRUARY 22, 1849

I packed my things early this morning and set off. The dining room of the inn was righted, the table back in place, and the mess of blood and glass cleaned off the floor. Only the empty shelf behind the bar remained as any reminder of what had occurred.

Heading out of town, I stopped at the general store. The shelves were almost bare. There stood on some of them glass jars full of nothing but air. Barrels and barrels were lined up against the walls with nothing inside them. Burlap sacks that might have once held grains and wheat now sagged down to the floor, empty. Everything I bought—dried beef, potatoes, and a few small onions—was expensive.

When I mentioned it to the storekeeper, he smiled. —There ain't nothing for a sensible man to get rich off of like another man's dreams.

I looked around. —I would think that would inspire you to keep better stocked.

He lost his smile. —You keep to your business; I'll keep to mine.

I walked north in the opposite direction I'd come into town. I saw some children playing in the dirt road by a house. One was a boy I'd seen the day before in the square. He wore the same shirt, and the blood had dried a dark brown on it. He seemed to be wearing it like a sheriff would wear his badge. He stood with his hands on his narrow hips, filled up with authority. After all, he had killed. I shuddered as I went by, feeling a hint of the nausea I had felt yesterday.

Just before the town tapered off into the nothing around it, I came across a church. It was built low to the ground, and its clay bricks appeared even more worn than all the other buildings. There was a bell in a steeple in the low, red roof of the building, but it looked as if it had been some time since it had rung. Two great crosses stood on either side of the bell. The door of the church was open.

I walked inside, my feet sounding loud on the packed dirt floor. I haven't ever had much of a relationship with God, other than to wonder at Him. Over the years, Joanna has tried to change my mind. She's a God-fearing woman, if not one of His most fervent worshippers. Many times she's asked me if I'm afraid to question God the way I do. Aren't I afraid what He'll do to me? Always my answer is the same. Of course I'm afraid of any God that could create a world such as the one we live in. Who could create a creature in His form that can act like the darkest of demons. Who wouldn't be afraid? But that fear doesn't equal reverence. There's holy and there's right, I would say, but that only seems half the picture God made. It is hard for me to put my feelings into words. But those feelings haven't much made me want to get down on my knees.

There were no windows in the church, just little open spaces by the roof covered over with bars that twined like briars. The inside was dark and as cool as a well. I could barely see in the shadows, but I began to make out shapes. There were statues all around me. A Virgin Mary with the saddest of looks in her upturned eyes stood near the door. Numerous cracks in the paint on her face and her robes showed the red clay beneath. Standing there gazing up to the black ceiling, she looked as if she'd been tortured some. And I guess that wasn't a bad way of describing what had been done to her.

Along the walls, in holders that went halfway up from the floor, were candles that burned in rows. Their light danced in random bursts, not reaching far beyond the areas of their yellow flames. They lit up the edges of the church and left the darkness in the center of the room steady. All that fire and all that blackness reminded me more of hell than heaven, more of a cursed place than a holy one.

There were wooden pews in two lines up and down the dim room. The wood, rubbed down smooth by years of use, was almost as dark as the middle of the church. How many people had knelt there, praying? And what good had it done, them now dead and their place of worship all but empty?

The longer I stood in the room, the less black the center of the church became. My eyes adjusted until I saw two women near the front, kneeling in one of the pews. I could see the backs of their heads, the flames of the candles reflecting in the shine of their black hair. I heard mutterings.

—Hello? I called out.

The heads did not turn.

My eyes adjusted further, and I noticed red and green and yellow cloth below the shining black of their hair. It was those two women selling beans and tortillas at lunchtime yesterday.

—*No molestar a ustedes, senoras*, I said. A compulsion had come upon me to speak to them. My mind stirred with a request, something foolish that their devout, kneeling forms had inspired.

The women did not turn. Their words came louder, as if they might drown me out altogether and make me disappear.

—*Me preguntaba . . .* , I stammered, not sure of my words and also sure the ones I was coming up with were foolhardy. —*Mi esposa . . . ella cree que como crees. Y si se puede decir una oración . . .*

I shook my head, the senselessness of what I was doing burning through my face. Surely I had not spoken in any clear way to them, any way they could truly understand. And surely they wouldn't be bothered with the requests of some man they had never met, who was as strange to them as they were to him. I was about to turn, to walk back into the day when one of the women stood.

With her long skirt brushing the dark floor, she walked over to a row of candles. In the dim light, she picked up one candle and touched its wick to a flame burning from another one. The second candle glowed yellow, its own flame growing and joining the other one, shining into the darkness, lighting the church just a bit more.

The second woman came into this light and kissed the first woman on the forehead, above and between her brows.

—Senora, I said, taking off my hat.

I walked into the light of day, a light so different than the one that had barely lit the church. But in that moment, the light of the sun seemed no more the work of God than the weak candlelight.

My dear,

This morning Mary came to the breakfast table with a bruise across her face. She did not speak of it, but Father asked about it as we sat down together. As Mary sputtered out a story of little Josephine hitting her by accident in a fit of anger, Nathaniel, so often a quiet and composed man, spoke somberly. —A woman must know her place.

He and Father exchanged hard looks as Father told him he would not abide by any man treating his daughter in such a way under his own roof. Nathaniel rose and stormed through the door of the kitchen, out into the yard beyond. Father rose, too, and followed him.

At the table, Mary folded upon herself in tears. She ran a hand over Josephine's small head and silken hair, but as she did so, we both noticed several new black patches. The child's hair had almost completely shifted in colors, and now instead of being blonde with streaks of black it was just bits of gold that shone through the color of pitch. This seemed to make Mary cry all the harder.

Across the room, Mother moaned. At first it was a sound we could almost disregard, as terrible as that may sound. Mother's moans are so frequent that we hear them in our dreams. With the constant exposure to them, they have lost the heartrending quality they once carried. So when her moans rose from the corner near the woodstove, we paid little heed. It was only when they became louder that I looked up from my futile attempts to comfort Mary.

Mother was standing there in her stained, threadbare nightclothes with her arms stretched out to us. She gave me such a start that I recoiled. Those arms had lost most of the meat on them, and it was as if she were reaching out with a skeleton's arms. Her nails had grown long and yellow, and they extended towards us like the points of knives on some deadly mission. Once I caught my bearings, I could hardly believe that I was thinking such uncharitable thoughts about my own beloved mother. The feeling of shame intensified as she gently laid those bony hands down on my and Mary's shoulders.

—Oh, Mother! Mother! we cried, jumping from our seats.

She stroked our hair as Mary had fondled Josephine's, calling us her dears. Our joy was great, so great I can barely fathom it now from the bottom of the well of despair I write you from.

—Come, she said, sitting with us. —Drink your tea. She reached out to the pot that sat in the center of the table, but her thin wrists were too weak, and her hands fluttered about the pot like small animals with broken backs.

Mary took the pot from her and poured the tea. As she did so, we heard Father and Nathaniel from the lawn. Their voices were like the echoes of drums and the sound of axes splitting wood—dull and resounding all at once. Mary's hands began to shake, and a stream of tea spilled over the edge of the cup. I rushed to clean it, then ran to the window and pulled the curtains tight across it. We could still hear their voices, but we could no longer see their forms out there, so alone in the wide open space with only their anger as a companion.

When I returned to the table, Mary was drinking tea with her shaking hands wrapped around her cup. She sipped mechanically, flinching as Father's and Nathaniel's voices rose above their low level into something higher and harder. Mother warmed her hands on the cup but did not drink. Her sunken eyes were soft on Mary. They turned to me then, too. So brown and gentle were they, like a doe's, that I lost myself for a moment, wondering what had happened to take my family away from its normal path of love and care and health and spirit.

Mary put her cup down, and before I knew it, Mother's weak, thin hand shot out and grabbed it. She swirled it to the left, quite violently, sloshing the leaves about the sides of the tan vessel. It was a trick Mother had been known to do when Father would tell some guest of her skill at tasseography, and Mother would have no hospitable choice but to show it. She had always been shy about it, but once she had begun she took the task quite seriously.

—Mother, you'll tire yourself, I protested.

But Mother swirled the leaves and then upended the cup, spilling out the liquid that Mary had left behind. Her eyes and her thin arms once again seemed frightening as she leaned over the table, focused on the small space inside that cup.

—A rain cloud I see there, she said. Her voice creaked like an old gate. —Leading into a storm as sure as I've ever seen one. It rips down a valley, paying no heed to what's in its way. You best take cover, my Mary. You best hide in these bushes I see over in this place, the ones splattered with the blood. And you best lift your feet so not to step in the pools of it. Do you see them on the ground?

—Mother! Mary shouted. She leaned to where Josephine sat, looking in amazement at her grandmother, and covered *the small child's ears.*

—Oh, you pretend you can't see the blood down there in yonder valley. You pretend that the gold shinin' atop it is all you see. And there it is, both blood and gold. And after that, beyond that, I see a bear. But it doesn't have brown or black eyes. Its eyes are yellow like a wild cat's. And its hands are the hands of a man. And it is pushing the stones out of the fire, my daughters. Pushing them hot and burning down towards us. Do you see those hot stones there, crackling? Burning like that bear's eyes? Do you see the blood all about you? You say you do not see it, that only I see it, but I know you do. I know you girls see the blood.

Mother looked down at the cup silently. It was then that spit started to pool at the side of her mouth and pour into the cup. The spit washed the leaves into a sodden mess at the bottom. All that saliva coming from her lips made it look as if her face were melting away, as if parts of her cheeks and chin were dripping into the cup. Mother closed her brown eyes. She was silent as Mary and I were silent. But then her lips parted one more time, and from them escaped these words. —I know you see the blood, my daughters.

Mother bent like a broken reed towards the cup. And at that moment, the door crashed inwards. Father came in, with splashes of blood across his face. He looked at us, not even making mention of Mother having risen from her bed, and looked away. He walked by us towards a bucket of water where he washed his face.

—Father! Mary screamed, rushing towards the door. —Nathaniel!

It was some minutes before Nathaniel walked in. His face was broken like a dropped melon. It was red as a sunset with blood and swelling.

Mother had been right in her predictions. See the blood we did. My dear, we did.

How has my family come to this? How is it that I am separated from you in the midst of all this ruin? What horrible fortunes are left for us—for my family and for you of whom I have heard nothing in so long? What else is the truth in what Mother has seen?

I sit in fear tonight of a monstrous beast with a man's hands in the nighttime just beyond my door. I dream back to Mother's face, melting away, it seemed, washing her visions right out of those clumps of leaves. If Mother saw the blood before we did, then perhaps she has seen this beast correctly as well.

My love for you remains great as my fear rises,
Joanna

FEBRUARY 23, 1849

When my thoughts turn to Joanna, no matter how these cooling days seep into my bones, I think warmth. I think fires and the heat of their orange and red flames sunk deep into them and heavy woolen clothes dried by them. I recall Joanna's fine hands by those fires as she taught me letters and words, tracing over the black marks I had always had such a time deciphering and making me understand them in a way that was smooth and clear. I remember those hands mending clothes or fashioning new ones. I think of them resting against her temples when she was doing hard thinking or working the numbers of what we had made and spent at the saloon. I can nearly feel those hands resting over my face when I told her of that night long ago, the night I struggle to keep down in my mind. The night that keeps coming back to me in bits and flashes as I walk along this northward trail.

But, no, I will not think of those memories I have done so well for so long to push away. Of those days that would have made me a different man if not for the sweet grace of the woman I met that night by the stream. Joanna.

I force my mind to a day when Joanna and I were together, back many years before we were married. She had always been independent, so for her to announce she would walk alone for an hour caused no disturbance, even when I began to court her formally. Of course, we would often meet in these hours, and in one of them, we stole away to a field. There was a hill there, soft and lush with green grass that rolled like a carpet cushioning our heavy steps. There, too, was a juniper that branched out so thick and provided a beautiful piece of shade. Under the tree we sat and watched the sun and the wind play in the valley like a gentle performance put on just for us. She did not go on and on talking, like some folk do, even when she was young. She watched the world about her with her soft, wide eyes and held on to my hand so gently.

—I don't need to say anything to you, do I? she asked after some silence. —I can just be here like this, and you'll understand somehow.

—I will always do my best to do so, I told her.

—I understand you, she went on. —In ways that don't need to be spoke of.

—There's parts of me that don't want to be understood, I suppose, and parts of me that do. I do believe you've got a good eye on most of the latter.

Though I was not expecting it—and to this day I know I was far from deserving it—Joanna leaned close to me and pressed her lips to mine. It was a soft, dry kiss, gone in an instant, but it lingered. For some time, we were lost in the closeness of one another, in the feeling of each other's breath. I had thought that perhaps we were from worlds too dissimilar, that I would surely be returning her father's hard looks and judgment were I not out to secure the affection of his daughter. But in that moment, those thoughts disappeared. We existed in a sort of limbo where the sky was her eyes, the earth her cheeks, and the oceans her lips. I swear I might be there to this day if not for a rumbling in the earth.

—Look! she cried.

A group of horses ran wild in the land beneath us. New as she was to the land, she was entranced as a child to see the sight. She squeezed my hand. It was then that I started to have a curious feeling. I lost track of where my hand ended and hers began. I wondered if maybe I could feel all the flesh, hers and mine, as if it were mine alone. It was a melting of sorts, a melding, as if we were metal heating and stirring and boiling together in a smelting cauldron. There was my arm, and then there was this space where our hands had been where the barriers of our flesh had now dissolved.

After a few moments, she pulled her hand away, and my hand once again became its own thing, familiar as it has always been. The spell was broken. But never once since then have I forgotten that feeling of oneness, of losing the edges of myself.

My Joanna. I wonder about her tonight.

FEBRUARY 24, 1849

My walking became steady. My feet ached in my boots, and I longed for the comforts of my home. But one foot fell in front of the other until I was carried farther and farther. The sun moved slowly; the wind carried dust motes by me in the shafts of sunlight that came through the branches. The words I would write in this journal rolled around in my head so that when I brought pen to page, I have thought the words many times already. I suppose this journey has changed me. And it has yet to reach the place it is going.

At dusk, I came upon a pool of water and a tall willow tree next to it, its branches cascading down like hundreds of tiny waterfalls. I thought I saw a shape, something human but somehow not right, against the thick bark at the base of the tree.

I approached carefully. It was a man, and his legs and torso were straight up against the tree. His body was upside down, bent near the neck, and his arms were splayed out directly on either side of him. His pose was unnatural, and I wondered how he could hold it. I came closer and noticed his eyes were almost closed, but the lids flickered so that the whites of his eyeballs showed every now and again. I paused, unsure of what to do. Finally, I stepped back and called out, —Hello?

The figure righted himself in a fashion too quick for me to follow. One moment he was inverted, the next standing there with his feet spread and legs beneath the rest of his body. The deep metal of a gun glinted at me in the growing darkness.

—I don't mean no harm, and I'm looking for no trouble, I said, raising my hands.

—A man could end up dead, startling another man that way out here, out where there ain't nothing to stop either of them from doin' what they will, he said. His voice was low and had a rumble to it that resounded with me. Then he lowered the gun, and a glint of gold winked through the dirt of his face.

My path, it appeared, had recrossed the Stranger's.

He tilted his head, his lips closing over the telltale gold teeth and his eyes narrowing. Those eyes seemed different, I thought. They might have been a different color than I remembered, or maybe they were set farther apart or closer together on his face. But there were those gold teeth glimmering and glinting. As I studied him, I got to feeling that those teeth knew me in some secret way. It was a feeling I couldn't rationalize but also one I could not shake. It was as if their glimmer were saying a slow hello to me.

—You have a familiar look about you, he said after staring me down.

—I believe our paths have crossed. You're tracking an Indian and some gold.

—You know my journey, he said. The Stranger folded a blanket that had lain near him into a tight square, then shoved his feet into his boots. He looked around, and I could swear that he lifted his chin and inhaled deeply through his nose, as if he were a wolf trying to pick up the scent of an animal it was stalking.

I walked over to the remnants of a fire in a circle of stones. Soon enough I would gather wood and build my own fire there, but for now I watched as the Stranger moved his halting way about, readying himself to find the Indian's trail.

As I kicked at the blackened pieces left in the fire pit, I saw something shining. I reached down and scooped it up, and, lo, it was a small piece of gold. Its surface ran smoothly into hollows and peaks, as if it had been poured into something and taken its time reaching the strange spots of that mold. It had an effortless look to it, a deep shine. It was like it spoke luxury with no words at all.

The Stranger glanced over at me. —You look surprised. Ain't nothing to be surprised about. The stuff is being found everywhere.

—I wonder if there's a vein of it under the very ground we stand on, I said. I didn't know what to do with that gold I held. After all I had seen, I didn't want to keep it. Yet I didn't want the Stranger to think anything odd if he saw me throwing it away. I walked over to where he stood and handed the piece to him. —You were camping this site first. I suppose that makes all that's found here yours.

The Stranger looked down at the gold in my hand with disdain, his lips drawing back, the gold of his teeth winking. He kept that expression until I withdrew my hand. I clasped the gold in my fist and lowered it to my side. The gold hung there, feeling hot and heavy, smooth and powerful.

—I ain't got no use for that.

I tried not to sound incredulous. —Aren't you seeking gold?

—I'm seeking gold, yes. But not that gold. The gold that was taken from me.

—But, sir, if you mined this very ground here, you might mine more and better. If there's gold to be found everywhere, I don't believe I understand why it matters *which* gold it is you find.

—You don't understand nothing! He angled his face towards me, and the veins stood out in his neck as if he were a snake about to strike. —That gold. It was my payment for all the hardness. My glory. It was like it was lyin' in the ground waiting for me. Singin' out to me. My right and my reward, what a decent man ought to get in this life. It ain't just no gold. Them pieces. Their shine, their gleam. They're mine. They was meant to be mine eternally. Almost like they was destined for my hands. I would know those pieces anywhere. I dream them at night, every last curve of them.

He nodded dismissively at me. —You take that gold. It ain't mine. What's mine is going to be found, not replaced. I'll know when I have it in my hand from the way it feels, the way it fits me, like the Lord made it to lie in my palm.

He turned away from me. As if to add the final word to the conversation, he made a sound in his throat and spat onto the ground.

The Stranger stuffed his blanket into his pack. He offered me another look of derision. —Mine this spot or move on. I don't care none. I got no rights to what's in the ground here. You might as well have it.

He stomped through the camp, his boots striking hard on the ground. His figure began to disappear into the night, his edges fading into the darkness until he was gone altogether. The night around the camp seemed darker for having him in it. Somewhere something howled. Maybe it was a coyote or maybe something else.

I dropped the piece of gold into my pocket and scrambled around for wood. I didn't much like being in the darkness the Stranger had left behind, and I rushed to build the fire that would disperse it. It wasn't until I had it glowing, until it seemed to fill the night more than the sound of the howls off in the distance, that I remembered the gold in my pocket.

I took it out and held it in my palm in the flicker of the fire. It seemed softer in that light, as if it glowed more naturally. The colors of the fire, the oranges and the reds, made the piece of gold seem warmer. For the first time since my journey started, I glimpsed the beauty in it. The Stranger had called it his "glory." And that seemed quite a name for it, a reward that had been promised long ago. Something for a man to strive for.

The more I stared at the gold, the more I saw all the toil of mankind. I swear I could almost see in that beautiful surface a scene of men swinging pickaxes, digging into the ground with shovels, moving saws, and straining their muscles. Hard, honest work, the kind of work that is oft taken advantage of by those high-up men who can't do the work themselves. Men laboring and sweating away to their deaths, struggling to feed families and build homes and at the same time making riches for other men.

And here in this piece of gold were all those things for the man who had earned them. What man wouldn't stop working for someone else's gain and scrabble for this gold nugget instead? A want sprung up in me, but it was more than want. More than desire. There was something right in it but not the kind of right that means "good." The kind of right that means "mine alone."

What if I stayed here, like the Stranger suggested? What if I mined this camp, washed dirt in the water of the lake, sorting out the pieces that shone from the pieces that were dark and dirty? What if I spent some time swinging a pick at the earth and sifting out the valuable from the worthless? What if I found a fortune? Joanna, it seemed, would wait for me if our future was to be safe and secure and helped along by riches. This strange journey, twined between the paths of the Indian and the Stranger, could work itself out in ways that had nothing to do with me. I could just stay here, making my fortune like any smart man would do.

Then the gold seemed to grow slightly heavier. Not anything different but somehow greater. "Swollen" is the only word for how it felt. And the oranges and the reds seemed to flicker deeper, like a fire in a hearth somewhere warm and comforting.

With a sharp breath, I clinched my fist over the gold. Hiding it from my view seemed to break my train of thought. It felt cold and small, locked in the flesh of my hand. But I knew I could not look at it again. I could not open even a finger of that fist.

I hurled the piece of gold in the direction of the pond. After a few seconds, I heard a plunk and nothing more. I listened and listened, but all I could hear was the rush of blood in my head.

FEBRUARY 25, 1849

When I awoke this morning, the sun was overhead, and the pond that had looked so calm and smooth in the dying light of yesterday was covered in a green scum that bubbled yellow in spots. In the middle of the pond was a break in the green scum, and inside that hole the water appeared black. The long branches of the willow tree I'd slept under became bare and black where they touched the water. I saw a few gaping mouths of fish come just above the surface and suck in the black water and green scum.

I shuddered at the sight, then packed my things and kicked at the fire pit to make sure the embers were all gone. But before I left the campsite, I sat down with my back against the willow tree. The thoughts of the night before lingered, no longer serious considerations in the daylight but ghosts of bad ideas that still peeked around the edges of my mind.

His "glory," the Stranger had called the gold. That gold inside the pouch of the Indian, that gold I'd seen cause so much trouble. His "glory."

The scum of the lake bubbled. I tried to tell myself it was the motion of a fish below the surface, but of that I was not sure.

Later

The sky is full of clouds, and the sun cannot be found. Every now and again I come across a tree that frightens me. They are of a kind I have never seen before. They have deep brown bark and reach up to the slate-grey sky with bare branches. They are devoid of anything resembling life or growth. These thick branches, empty and forlorn, break off into fingers that reach up and up, as if clawing. As if straining for something they will never close over. They are dead, these trees, but still they reach, like spirits that left behind something valuable and want it back. I can almost hear them growing, reaching farther even in their death.

I do not know why these trees have lost their leaves or why I see more of them as I walk on, no matter how far I go. Each time I see another, I receive a shock to my system, a deep jolt that spreads into my bones. I imagine my bones blackened like the branches of these trees. While I shake inside, each tree stands there as stark as a sentinel. But what they watch for, I cannot fathom.

Later

I came across a camp of four men tonight. Three of them wore felt hats that were beaten down a bit by the weather and the sun. Their clothes had rips and holes, especially around the knees and elbows, which were also stained with the brown of dirt that had been ground in deeply. One of the men wore all deerskin, and his clothes seemed to have fared less poorly in the streams and the dirt. At the edge of their camp, two mules and two horses grazed slowly.

As I approached, the men were setting about some domestic tasks. The man in all leather stirred a three-legged pot over the fire, throwing in pinches of this and that from little sacks near the fire pit. The other men were spreading out blankets, taking off boots, clearing rocks, and stacking them up around the edges of the fire.

One man, the youngest with the round cheeks of a child, brushed down one of the horses. He fed it something, perhaps a lump of sugar, out of his hand. After a while, he turned to the man in leather at the fire. —You need help there with dinner?

—Now, you know that ain't right, another man said. —You know we take turns, and tonight is his turn. Terrible at it or not, he's gonna make us our dinner. That's just the way it operates.

Frowning, the man in leather threw bits and pinches of things into the pot with more force.

—You men got room around that fire for one more? I called out. —I'll help best as I can with whatever needs to be done.

The men all turned towards me at once. They eyed me up and down, taking in my clothes and my boots and the gun that hung at my side.

—I suppose he looks all right, the man in leather finally said to the others.

I could tell he was the leader among them, despite the talk about the cooking he was doing. Once he had accepted me, the others let their hard gazes fall away, and when they looked at me again, their eyes were not as probing.

I stepped up to them, getting a strange feeling about me, a feeling that they were familiar but not. That I had met them before, though where I could not remember. I shook my head. It seemed the fog of my path had gotten inside it. —Where you men heading to? I asked by way of clearing my head.

—I ain't interested in idle talk about destinations, the man by the fire said. —There's a well down that path, all covered up. Why don't you make yourself useful and water down them animals?

—All right, I said. I went to where another man was holding a bucket and took it from his hands.

Then I walked down the path, stumbling over rocks in the blackness that was pure and unbroken ahead of me. The campfire floated like a wraith behind me, dancing between the trees, its light taunting me. I almost tripped over the well, which was set halfway in the path itself. I felt around with my hands to discover the covering and removed the boards. By feel, I positioned the bucket over the hole and lowered it. It seemed to go down for an eternity. Something crept into the edges of my mind. The story that man who was killed a few days ago at the inn had told me about the shade of a woman wandering the night. I have never believed in such things. But out here in the darkness with those four men far away, I kept my eyes trained towards the firelight. The sound of the bucket splashing into the water finally reached me. I let it sink, then pulled it up, hand over hand.

I made four trips, bringing a bucket to each animal. The horses and the mules were grateful for the water. They lowered their heads gracefully to the bucket, their sad, large eyes remaining above it, staring at me. Those gentle animal eyes, the eyes of creatures too domesticated to survive out on their own, beholden to the kindness of men, made the trips back and forth to the well seem less dark.

By the time I was finished, the man in leather was serving dinner. I went to my pack and drew out my metal plate, heading towards the pot.

The pot was full of beans, but when I sat down to taste them, they were like no beans I had ever eaten before. They were far too salty, and I'm not sure what else the man in leather had put in them, but they were bitter, too. Each bite made me want to drink a bucket of water myself. I ate spoonful after spoonful, telling myself I was lucky to have anything. But I did not feel so very lucky.

I glanced around at the other men. Judging by the looks on their faces, they were no happier. I regarded the man in leather. He was trying not to look displeased, but with every bite his face puckered as if he were biting into a lemon. There was silence around the campfire.

—Damn it, you can ruin anything, one man said finally, throwing what was left on his plate into the fire. —I'd rather eat just about anything. What comes out of that mule's ass probably tastes better than this.

The other men, except the man in leather, broke into laughter and emptied their plates into the fire. It hissed and popped for a moment.

—Guess you're going to have to cook after all, one of the men said to the young man with the clear face.

He smiled and blushed and said that of course he wouldn't mind cooking. In fact, he had been preparing for such an occasion, just in case. There were still plenty of beans left soaking, and if the men would give him a bit of time, he would have dinner ready. He stood and took the three-legged pot off the fire, the handle wrapped in leather. He grabbed a shovel and dug a hole away from the campfire and poured the terrible pot of beans into it before covering it over.

Now the young man scurried around the campfire. He went out to the well and poured more water into the new batch of beans he had placed in the pot. He removed a small dried pepper like the Mexicans cook with and a piece of what looked like salted pork from a bag. The pot simmered over the campfire, the fire licking the edges and bubbles beginning to show.

As the young man became absorbed in his work, the other men relaxed, sitting near the fire and talking.

The man in leather seemed to have gotten over any embarrassment rather quickly and spoke to the other men with authority once more. —All these difficulties that arise when women ain't about. Who would have thought, back home in the East, all the things that would have to be done without them.

—That's true, another man said. —My clothes wouldn't

never be in this state if my ma were here. God knows I've never walked around in clothes that need darning in my entire life.

The third man shook his head. —If that's all you miss women for, darned clothes and good food, then you men ain't got the experience or the imagination to know what women are best for.

—You ain't never been close enough to a woman to know what's done with her, the man in leather said. — Don't go talking as if you have.

The other man's face got hard in the light of the fire. —Don't suppose you know what I've done or not done, in addition to not knowing much about the sweets of society.

The argument escalated. First one man's face went ugly, then the next followed suit. Their words got harder and harder. Their hackles raised like a dog that sees a stranger. I began to think their fight was about something more than experience with women, maybe about the injured pride of the man in leather. He was the first to remove his sidearm from his belt. Soon both men had their guns drawn and were waving them something fierce.

The other men ducked and dove out of the paths of their barrels. I, too, moved out of the way. I hoped the night would not end in bloodshed.

After some time of threatening and waving, a man from the sidelines stepped between them.—Now, men! Now, men! There ain't no use acting this way. Just because we ain't in a civilized place don't mean we have to act like barbarians.

The two men lowered their guns but eyed each other with fire.

I went over to the youngest man to see if I might help him and be away from the anger of the other men.

—No, good sir, you just let me take care of things. I'm the best cook around this fire, and if we had to start dinner again we'd be here until morning. In fact, I best stay back tomorrow from digging and make us some sourdough from a little starter yeast I've begun.

He went on stirring and seasoning, as if the fight hadn't even taken place. It seemed to calm the other men.

We resettled around the fire, and one of the men got to telling a tale. It was a dark and eerie one with people but a foot and a half tall working together to carry off a man much bigger caught alone out in the land. The story took many twists and turns, with the man's body finally being found in the desert, picked clean. It wasn't the best of tales waiting for supper, but the men relaxed even more, easing down from their fighting moods.

It didn't seem too long before dinner was ready. Beans and potatoes and some raw onion and it tasted as good as anything I've ever eaten.

—You should have seen me trade for that onion at the last outpost, the young man said. He was swollen up with pride.

The other men laughed.

—You'll make a fine wife to somebody someday, boy, the man in leather said, winking at the youngest man.

All the men laughed even more, and the youngest one, at whose expense the joke was told, joined in.

After dinner, the man in leather requested a song. One of the others took out his banjo and picked and strummed at it, making it ring in the way that only a banjo can. There is something about a banjo that sounds forlorn in the darkness of night, with the shadows jumping all about.

The youngest man sang in a low, sweet voice.

> *You'll find your treasure in life after,*
> *You'll find your treasure, dear man,*
> *For life is as cruel and unkind as the sea,*
> *And your treasure's as warm as the sands.*
> *Your treasure ain't in no diamonds,*
> *Your treasure ain't no jewels,*
> *For all these great worldly riches*
> *Are merely the riches of fools.*

The men around the fire shifted during the song. I suppose they might have liked it in their old lives of toil, but out here, where they felt so sure of getting all the riches they desired, the lyrics did not suit them. The youngest man paid no mind, however, just kept singing in a voice so sweet it reached out and pulled the blanket of the night tight around the fire. When his words ceased, the fog settled even closer than the twilight blue of the evening. It rose like spirits from out of the very air. The men glanced around, but I could see them do so for only a little while before they were gone in the fog. I noticed here and there a hand, a nose, a cheek, but mostly the men were lost around the fire. Then there was just a little globe around the fire of clearness, and beyond that, opaque night. We shifted in it, wondering.

FEBRUARY 26, 1849

A man joined the camp this morning, helloing through the trees as I had last night. He appeared among the greenery, taking his hat off as if the campsite were a church he was stepping into. His hair was sandy brown, and his mustache had never grown in proper, despite him being old enough that it should have. It hung down over his lip in wisps.

—Hello, gentlemen, he said. He clasped his hat to his bony chest. —Many men call me a friend or companion but not on this trail. I am searching for traveling partners as I make my way in this great wild world of ours, or, barring that, would like to join you for a bit of food to fill the longing growing in my belly.

One of the men at the campsite whooped at the ornate talk. —Well, listen, Companion, he said, lacing the final word with insincerity, —we're a mining outfit. We ain't looking for no new friends.

I stepped away from the men, slinging my pack over my shoulder. There was something about this man that did not sit right with me, but I had begun to get lost on the trails. Sometimes in a real sense, mixing north with west and west with south, but sometimes in a quieter way that had to do with the rocks and the trees and the mist and the fog, the direction inside my own mind. The fog that had rolled in last night, blinding us, had dissipated at dawn, but it had yet to leave the inside of my skull. Perhaps a traveling companion wouldn't be the worst thing for me.

—Where you heading? I asked.

—North a ways, he said. —To San Francisco at least and mayhap farther. A man doesn't rightly know his destination until he finds it, wouldn't you agree, sir? A man might wander this beauty-laden sphere of an earth his whole life, and still his true and final destination eludes him until a shining time comes when—

—Listen, Companion, one of the men said. —We are packing up camp, and I suggest that if you're going, you best be on your way instead of making big speeches about nothing.

The Companion bowed, clutching his hat to his chest even more tightly. —You seem a man who knows business is business and chatter is chatter. He turned to me. —Sir? If you be heading north a way, perhaps our paths may intertwine for but a brief moment in the scheme of all things. Have you heard of this fine and resplendent city of San Francisco?

—Here and there, I said, —but nothing has made it seem like somewhere worth stopping.

—Oh, but much has changed. The city's become downright cosmopolitan. I do hope you will accompany me within its boundaries, for wealth and riches can be found there that one cannot lay eyes on even in the gold fields.

—My path isn't a strict one, I said.

—A strict path, I always say, my dear fellow, is truly a foolhardy one. Once a man sets out to go to a place, he loses the myriad of other places he might find along the way to that unambiguous destination. On the other side of the equation, a man who lets a path find him—why, he is a man who is genuinely blessed with the gifts that peregrination has to offer.

He swung his arm up at his side and placed his hat back upon his head. He extended his arm out towards the path I had walked down on my way to the well. —Let us go forth, kind fellow, to the delights that our wayfaring may take us to!

The men at the camp chuckled, but I walked along that path before this strange new Companion.

That is how we set out together, the Companion spinning tales of what it would be like in San Francisco. Though I assured him I wasn't interested in women or drink, he kept up with talk of them and other pleasures that might be found there. His talk was grandiloquent, and I wondered how he had survived run-ins with other men who might be less obliged to listen to his flowery words. But there was something slick about him that made me sure he'd been able to glide away from any trouble.

His talk filled up my head, and I suppose I was right in that it wouldn't leave room for the confusing and careening thoughts that had snuck into my mind in the past days in the fog. The trees were just trees, not the wraiths I had witnessed the day before. The rocks were just rocks, the dirt just dirt. I walked and walked, drifting on the wave of his ornate words.

FEBRUARY 27, 1849

The Companion goes on and on as we walk. He talks about the history of the territory of California, the trees we see and the animals that cross our path, the boom that he believes is coming and its benefits, the future of machines, the various virtues of women he has known and the failings of women who have rejected him, the opportunity found in this place called America.

The only topic he seems mum about is himself. I have yet to learn from where he has come, what his history and past hold, what things brought him here, or what he has left behind. He is a blank slate that is nevertheless full of words. Trying to engage him in any of these topics is like trying to grab a reflection in the water. The minute you reach out to make it real and solid, it splinters and skates away.

—Where are you from? I asked as we picked our way over a field littered with rocks that threatened to twist our ankles at every step.

—Seems less interesting to think about where we're from than where we're going, wouldn't you agree? he said.

—Mankind seems to indeed be progressing towards what is good and what is condign. We are erecting cities and acquiring scholarship and discovering more and more. We are taming that which is wild in our very own beings and in the uncultivated world around us. We are making beauty and we, ourselves, every generation, are moving more towards what is sublime. I do believe, though you may think me touched of mind, that one day mankind will conquer the very stars in the sky. Many men have thought me crazy for saying so. And if crazy is a belief in what man can accomplish with his angelic hands, I am happy, good sir, to be a madman.

And so the conversation veers away from all topics pertaining to him like a silverfish. He does not ask me for my opinions on what he says. It is just as well. Still, despite his grand words, at times I catch something in his eyes that I cannot fully pin down. Something that slides away as smoothly and freely as his words slip from his lips, leaving just the final lash of its tail to prove it was ever there at all. And at these times, I feel a shudder within myself.

FEBRUARY 28, 1849

Yesterday the Companion and I came upon the motion of water, but no water was to be seen. The wooden hulls and white sails of boats rose there instead, cloaking even the light of the sun where it was reflected in the bay. There was hardly space to breathe between them. They crowded between the gentle risings of green land at the edges of the bay like the spires of fancy churches. I have seen boats gliding in slow and smooth on the water before, but never had I seen so many stopped, swaying gently, taking up so much space, and foretelling this many people and supplies. We walked down towards them as if coming upon a wonder.

—Here we are, sir, the Companion said, waving his hat towards the crowded bay. —We have arrived at last at this city of every delight to be found on the earth. A man can tell just by looking that he will never want in a metropolis like the one before us.

For once his words seemed correct. There was so much of everything that the stream of it seemed to surround and carry me. Men of every color, talking to each other with gestures and odd smatterings of languages of all kinds. Tall men, short men, men in fancy clothing, men who were in shirts and boots like myself.

I looked down at my own form, and for the first time I felt the dirt where it had collected on my flannel shirt, smelled the pungent aroma from the boots I had worn in dirt and water alike. I felt like a stranger wandering in from another land. But then I glanced about and realized there were too many strangers for anyone to pay any mind.

A little man with a curled mustache grabbed my hand. He spoke to me in a flowing language as he gestured at my boots, then the rags and polish and chair nearby. He tried to pull me towards them, saying, —Monsieur, monsieur. But I broke away.

It was about noontime when we came into the city proper, and all around us bells started ringing. They reverberated off the wooden buildings, becoming muffled as their noise bounced down the cloth tents. I looked around to see the church steeple they were coming from, but there didn't seem to be any churches.

Men poured into saloons and restaurants and sat around tables that were set up with cards and games. Gold appeared from every hand to fall onto the ground and shine, with nobody bothering to pick it up. It scattered across tables, changing hands so rapidly that you could barely tell whose was whose. Things started moving too fast, and everything around me began to run into everything else—hands into arms into tables into faces into gold.

I knew rightly that the world couldn't be moving that

fast, but still I had to look away, back to the bay, back to the boats that rocked slow and steady. It was then that I noticed a body on the wharf, splayed out on its back, with dead eyes rolling up to the sun. Men were stepping around it as if it weren't even there.

—Come on, the Companion said, pulling my hand as the bootblack had tried to. —I got gold dust, and there's gambling to be done right here and now.

He led me to a table where the pieces of gold were piling high around the flashes of black and red and white that were playing cards. A Mexican man was behind the table, snapping the cards down on the black felt that covered it with an expert flip of his wrist. His hard expression did not change whether he won or lost money.

Standing across from him at the table was a small man dressed not much different than me. It seemed he had come from the mining prospects by his baggy pants and dirty cotton shirt and the slouching hat pulled down over his eyes. He was young, with hair not yet growing on his face. His eyes danced, sparkling in a way I have rarely seen. When he won and gold was pushed towards him, his smile—flashing like quicksilver across his face, full of straight, shining teeth—was something to marvel at.

I wasn't the only one staring at this young man. The Companion was looking at him, too, his eyes sharp.

The young man kept winning and winning, some wonderful luck making the pile of gold in front of him grow and shine. The shine seemed to get brighter as the pile grew until it was like a ray of sun falling directly on it. The pieces of gold were varied, some as small as a speck of sand, some big shimmering hunks, their surface as uneven as the ocean waves. The face of the young man receded behind the shine of it, and it became hard to tell if the Companion was staring at him or the gold. The sharp look in the Companion's eyes had turned to something burning and smoldering.

Between his look and the shine of the gold, I felt as if there were a magnifying glass between the sun and us at the table. I wondered if the whole thing would burst into flame right then and there and all of us, too. The heat under my collar rose, and I yanked at it, seeking to get cool air back onto my skin. Everything felt closer. I had to step away. I found myself pressed against a building, gasping for air.

The city swirled around me again. As many white canvas tents rose as buildings, giving the streets a brighter feel. A tall man in a fine suit with black hair and deep-set eyes exited one of these tents. He raised his hands and shouted for all to come inside and see the show that was about to begin.

A woman, looking even finer than the man, her white dress dripping with glass beads that caught the light of the sun and turned it to little rainbows across the fabric, came out next to him. Without warning she took the slightest step back and opened her mouth. Out of her throat came the most beautiful singing I have ever heard. Better than sparrows and fuller than an entire church choir. She stood there handing it out to any passerby who chose to turn his ear her way. A few did, but most went on without troubling themselves over it as she sang, her voice reaching up, then coming down low all of a sudden like a bird shot out of the sky and plummeting. She stretched out her hands, too, inviting.

As I watched her, I didn't quite take notice of how her voice was getting inside me. I'm not sure what I mean by that, because I couldn't feel it until it began to shake things up. Then, before I knew what was happening, tears were running down my face.

I stumbled across the street towards her outstretched arms, as if she were a mother and I was nothing but a crying child. The sun and the street and the people and the languages seemed to fade, and there was just her white gown with its prism beads. I could barely see her face behind her wide-open mouth, and I wasn't sure if she was American or Mexican or European or Celestial. I walked into a man who shoved me hard and who may have pulled his gun, but I was too focused on her to care. I wove in and out of the stream of people, bashing and forcing like a salmon swimming upstream. Black boots pounded the dirt around me. Silver belt buckles flashed. Tobacco-stained teeth appeared behind snarled lips. Then all of it faded from view.

I was close to her when I felt hands grab my arms. Still, I didn't see anything but her. But the hands righted me, and I was staring into the face of the man who'd been announcing the show.

—You want to buy a ticket? he asked. He gave me a shake.

My brain seemed to slap around in the dry socket of my skull. The sun was beating down hard. The woman's mouth closed, and her face reappeared, her brown eyes warm.

—A ticket? he asked. —A ticket?

The woman backed into the tent. I could hear other

voices, higher and lower than hers, tripping up and down scales, coming from inside.

The tall man shook me harder than I would have expected from someone dressed so finely. —It's a show, you cur. A show. There's women for what you're looking for all over. Now either buy a ticket and keep your hands clear or go the hell to the kind of places where women let you grab them and slobber your damned snot all over them.

My senses started coming back to me a bit. The white of the great tents filled my vision. I felt another pair of hands grab me.

—Where you been at? What kind of trouble are you getting yourself into?

I turned and saw the Companion, giving a hard look to the tall man in the suit who had my other arm.

—You best watch your friend before he ends up dead. This ain't the mines and the camps you're in no more.

—You mind yours, and I'll mind mine, the Companion said. He opened his mouth, taking in a deep breath, and I suspected he was about to launch into some more of his grandiloquence. But then his mouth snapped shut, and he pulled me in the direction he'd come from.

I still felt a bit shaken, and the ground beneath me did not seem solid. It was as if I were walking on waves.

—You sly old scoundrel, he intoned in my ear. —All that talk about not looking for women. (Here, he took on what I presumed was an imitation of my voice.) —I have me a wife, and those women in San Francisco can't tempt me any. You talk and talk, but then the first woman you find—

hell, not even a woman in the market, the first woman you look at—and you're crawling after her, making her man angry. Well, don't you worry yourself any, my good friend. If it's women you're after, women we'll find for you. But first I have to win back some of the money I lost at the last table.

We moved from table to table. Each was presided over by a brown-skinned man, each held piles of gold rather than anything resembling coins. I had to focus on the cards, for when I focused on the faces of the men playing, odd things happened. Their foreheads or noses grew longer, their lips flatter. Their eyes became pools. If they opened their mouths, the darkness inside became endless like the sky with no stars.

The Companion dragged me from table to table, but it was all the same. Something seemed to have come loose in my head, was rushing away. I focused on the red hearts, the black clubs. Only they stayed steady, stark against the white background of the cards.

The Companion won a considerable amount, then took me to an inn where we ate all the food we could hold down. The Companion passed gold to the innkeeper to pay for us both. The table in front of me was something to focus on, for the world around me still swam. I felt sick, not from the motion of everything but from the notion that nothing was just what it was. Everything could become anything any-time. There didn't have to be any warning, and, likely, there wouldn't be.

We went back to the tables where the card games were being played. I couldn't focus on strains of the chorus around me so well, and often the swells of words coming from the Companion were notes in the greater arrangement, ones I could not hear as separate. I lost most of what he was saying. I watched other men laugh and scowl at him, but always I had to look away.

The sun sank below the buildings and tents, and lights came up around us. The white tents glowed like heavenly things, lit up yellow by the lanterns inside. They blocked out any light from the moon or the stars, so bright were they. It calmed me a bit, that light. It was something I didn't have to focus on too hard. It was just there looking warm all around me. The faces around the tables grew less stark, too, and took on tones of orange and yellow. The shadows on those faces were softer. I was able to raise my eyes again.

The men around me smiled and grimaced, laying down their gold. They had all kinds of faces, and those faces were solid. The yellow skin and dark eyes of the Celestials. The shining mahogany skin and black hair of Negroes, free in this setting as they wouldn't be in other parts. Men from places I didn't recognize, some with fire in their eyes, some tattooed, some wearing wraps on their heads, some Indians wearing little at all but still producing gold to set down on the table.

Then the young man with sparkling eyes reappeared, edging up to the gambling table where we stood. He scooped gold out of a bag that seemed heavy and fat, then put it down on the table.

His motions were so graceful that all the men—no matter what their dress or the color of their skin or the shape of their eyes or face—stopped to watch. Many of them looked away, as if ashamed. In their eyes had been a spark and a longing for that grace, something they must have felt they had to conceal. The men parted a bit, giving the young man with the shining eyes room at the table.

He laid down more of his gold. He barely spoke to the other men around him, and when he did, it was in a quiet voice that was almost a whisper. But his face—his broad smile, his dancing eyes, the way he pursed his lips in consternation the few times he lost a bit—spoke volumes. But largely, luck seemed to be with him.

The other men looked churlish as their piles shrunk and his grew. And yet they could not keep their eyes off the way he reached out and scooped in their gold.

—Damned beginner's luck, the Companion growled. —He ain't nothing but a baby, and there he is, raking it in.

The Companion seemed to have been affected by the boy's presence in more ways than one. He shoveled out his own gold, each bet larger than the last, as if he knew he would score back enough to make up for all his folly. But that time never happened. His face fell deeper and deeper into a dark scowl as the young man's joy and money grew.

Then the Companion had nothing. He turned his leather bag upside down over the table and shook it. Not a speck of gold fell from it.

—Move along, the Mexican behind the table said in perfect English. He had not spoken a word in the time we'd been here. —Move along. No space for you here. There's only room for men with gold to gamble.

The Companion drew back, and I drew back with him. I thought we would head to another place, but there we stood in the dark just far enough from the lighted tents that shadows played all over our faces. There we stood watching the table, watching shadows fly between us and the lantern lighting up the cards. There we stood listening to men whoop in joy or groan in disillusionment. We stood there, watching.

After some time, I saw the young, bright-eyed man withdraw from the table. Again, the men around him parted and gave him a wide berth to walk through. His bag of gold was visible at his side, bulging like to break. He walked, light and sure, down the road.

—Come along, the Companion said.

We followed the young man, not close enough so that he would notice us but not far enough that the crowd would swallow him up. He paused here and there to peer into a building. Finally, a saloon beckoned him into its black doorway.

The Companion turned to me. —I am not a man to hold count of the favors I have done for other men. As I always say, give when you can, and avoid at all costs making another man feel beholden to you for it. But now I find myself with no money left to speak of and a throat dryer than a desert at noontime. And as I bought you a fine meal earlier this evening, I was wondering if you wouldn't find the kindness to take me into that there bar and help me quench my thirst, even though you yourself are not a drinking man. It would be most humbly appreciated, my good friend, and as soon as I win back what I lost today, your benevolence will be repaid a hundredfold.

There did not seem any way I could refuse him.

We entered the saloon. The light from the lanterns on the walls jumped and danced, making the room seem closer and warmer. A few men who had clearly been enjoying their drink for some time were dancing with one another, linking arms and twirling around, though the only music was drifting in from outside the bar. They grasped one another's arms and slapped at their own thighs and roared in laughter. Around them, men were drinking and talking, and men were hiding out at low tables in dark corners, bottles and glasses in front of them. Men were leaning close, making plans, dreaming aloud. The young man from the gambling table had found a bottle and a table and now sat observing the scene around him.

I passed the bartender enough money to buy a small bottle for the Companion. As I waited, I glanced down the bar at the crowd of men and felt a strong longing for my own life. This world, running away and altering itself always, is too much for me. I longed to escape into my dim saloon.

But standing here, I doubted I would ever find the calm of my own life again. Things have changed. The gold has brought men, and the men have brought a fever. And that fever burns hot with their dreams and desires. There won't ever be a day like they think, where everything is ease and riches and nobody's left to account for it. But I could tell and tell them, and still they would come out here to look. Still the quiet and the ease and the dimness I once had would be lost and gone. All for the hopes of an easy payday.

The Companion took us to a table across the room from the young man where we could still clearly see him. The young man's face contorted every time he took a sip, a grimace that made him somehow look even more delicately made than he had all night. He was not a man built for drinking, I could tell. Yet there he was, making himself do it, watching the men who were made for nothing *but* drinking sway and clomp around him.

The Companion began to hold forth on the history of whisky. —Made in its original form by Italian alchemists and adopted by monks as a cure for smallpox, he said. —Then the Irish started to experiment, to scientifically ponder other kinds of fermentation. The first to drink whisky was a holy man, and damned if that holy man didn't almost see God. The drink went on to kings and was as fit for the monarchs as for the men of God.

But as he went on and on, I noticed that his attention never wavered from the young man who had won so much at the gambling table. His eyes had a sharp, wolflike look in them. As if they were hungry for something.

His words became slower and slurred together a bit. He reveled in them, thinking them grander and fuller. I have seen men's self-importance swell from alcohol many a time and knew the signs of it. He gestured with his glass, as if giving a speech. Then, abruptly, his glass clinked down against the table.

I looked across the room. The young man was heading towards the door. I looked back and saw the Companion pick up his bottle and drink directly from it, finishing the whisky off in a single gulp. He stood up, making the bottle and the glass clatter. He started towards the door. I followed.

Back into the night we went, and the white tents with their yellow lights now shone like holy things. In the wooden buildings and in the alleys between them were shadows that jumped and lingered and grew thick and deep. The Companion rushed down the street, apparently not caring if the young man saw him. I rushed after him.

The young man seemed to have taken his whisky hard. He swayed and stumbled over his own feet. His bag of gold bounced against his leg, and pieces of it tumbled out and to the ground. At first the Companion stopped to pick them up but then let them lay there, shining.

We passed the young man on a dark spot of the roadway in a row of wooden buildings with dim lanterns hung outside them. The Companion pulled me into an alleyway. The shadows of the building fell all around us, and I was not sure that the figure on the road was the same young man we had followed, for his face was shaded and dark. I could not see his eyes or cheeks; his mouth was nothing but a dark slash.

The Companion nudged me. —Call him so I can give him back his gold.

—Here, you. Over here.

I stepped farther into the alley as the young man stopped and peered into the shadows. His face was wholly obscured, and I could only see his body. His shoulders slouched under the weight of drunkenness and looked even more so like the thin shoulders of a child. There was nothing to his body. A stiff wind could have snapped him. He stepped hesitantly towards the alley.

Shadows moved in flashes. I thought I saw something shine. I watched swift movements that could have been arms, hands. I heard a grunt, then something muffled like a lady's scream. It was cut off, as if a hand had been placed over a mouth. What must have been a hat flopped to the ground. In the shadows, I saw that thin frame and hair that flowed and shone coming down over slumped shoulders.

And a voice was throaty and grunting like an animal. —Fooled all the rest, didn't ya?

Figures on the ground then. I walked out of the alley, and the dim light of a lantern fell on the forms there. I saw a body holding down another body, heard the rip of clothes. I saw the soft mountains of small breasts against pale skin. And on top of that skin dark clothes and arms flailing and something flashing.

—Bitch. Deceiver. Bitch.

A scream again, cut off. A body jerking up and down and half dragging in the mud. I saw a flash of the Companion's face, the expression that accompanied his smooth and fine words gone. He wore a look of pure hatred and malice.

The face of the person on the ground, the person who had looked like a young man but now seemed to be a woman, was still in the shadows, still hidden, blocked so perfectly that it was like she wore a mask made of darkness. On the ground her shadow seemed to move in ways her writhing body did not, pulling this way and that as if it were trying to escape.

I moved towards them, their shapes. A flash of knife glinted towards me in a ray of light from some lantern. Thinking, *Joanna*, I ran.

I fled down the street, those grunts and cries and moans following me, even when I could no longer hear them. The word "deceiver" echoed in my ears or maybe throughout my head—I could not tell the difference anymore. Hanging heavy in my mind were my own words, the words that had preceded the struggle. *Here, you. Over here.* It was I who had called her over to her grim fate. Far and fast as I ran through streets, through bodies of men, I could not escape that.

I ran until my breath came in jagged bursts, burning my lungs. My throat felt raw from gasping. I stopped, bent over, one hand on my thigh and one on my chest. Even when the torment of the sharp breaths ceased, I could not escape the other torment caused by the role I had played in the crime. All around me, the city seemed to be going on as usual, as if what I had seen in the alley had been a dream or a delusion, not something real involving the hurt of someone living, breathing.

I stood there trying to think, but thinking only led me to the certainty that I might as well be as guilty of the crime as the Companion. And to compound my guilt, I had done nothing to help the woman. I had lured her into the shadows, then run the other way when the Companion attacked her. I could not help thinking of my wife. Not only did I think of how such a thing might well happen to Joanna but of how she would feel if she knew what I had done in that shadowed alley. I pictured her brown eyes flashing like angry lightning. Then her looking away from me, not to look back. Were a mirror nearby, I would not have been able to gaze at my own reflection.

After I was able to breathe again, I hurried back in the direction I had come from. Minutes had passed, but the woman could still be lying there, needing my help. A part of me knew that I should not return to the place where I had helped commit the crime. That preservation side felt strong in a way it had not in years. And the old days, the dark days, were piling into my mind, burning hot. Only my task at hand kept them at bay. Even the thought of Joanna had abandoned me. As it should have. Someone as base and foul as me had no right using thoughts of someone like her to comfort himself.

The more I walked, the less the disagreement between my thoughts seemed to matter. All forms of lawlessness seemed to be happening around me in the night streets. Fights and rowdiness and prostitutes looking for work. It bothered me deeply that I might be the only one who cared about what had happened in the alley. That others might shrug and think it was just part of a night in San Francisco.

I thought I saw her everywhere—in every slight man stumbling a bit, in every woman dressed for the night, and even in people who were not of her race, who were not near her age, who looked not the least bit like her. Everyone's eyes seemed to shine the way hers had. I wanted to grab people who passed me by to ask them if they were all right, if they had been hurt, if they needed my help.

I discovered several spots where the crime might have occurred. I hunted for signs of scuffle in each alley. For spots of blood or for fallen gold, for long hairs or clothing that had been ripped away. I looked for a body. But I found nothing.

It was some time before I gave up the search. I had edged into an alley and was on my knees scanning the ground. I thought I felt the imprint of a body. But whatever had made that imprint was gone. And then for a moment, I was not there but in a foul day and a hopeless time, seeing a body splayed on the ground.

I jerked back into the present. I caught my breath and leaned against the wall of a building. I drew my knees up to my chest and wrapped my arms around them. I placed my head down on the dirty knees of my pants. There was nothing I could do to change what had happened or the part I had played in it. All of it. Any of it. Past or present.

I sat there for a while wallowing in the bad feeling that had come over me. I listened to the roar of the night around me. Then there seemed but one thing left to do.

In the closest saloon, I poured a bottle of whisky down my throat as if to put out a fire there. It hit me hard. The singing of the men around me swelled. I screamed for them to shut their mouths. I was in no mood for song. Before long, my fists were swinging in the dim light. I did not feel the fists that fell upon me. I did not feel it when I was thrown into the nighttime street. I did not feel lucky to have kept my life.

I stumbled, a formidable presence, through the door of an establishment run by Celestials. They seemed so fine and

mannered, offering me food. I told them I had seen what
had been done to people like them. They looked at me with
something that might have been sympathy but was probably
just them being good at their business. As they delicately
took up sticks to eat, I shoveled food into my mouth. I do believe I wept and apologized to them, for myself and for others.
I recall thinking how far from enough my words were.

I gambled at a table, the only one throwing down coins.
My coins must have seemed nothing to the men dealing the
games, yet they let me stay. I howled with losses and roared
with wins. The men around me seemed like companions,
but then they were not. I upended a table spread with gold.
The gold rolled onto the dirt street, and the men all scrambled after it. I laughed at them clawing at the ground. I
laughed, and away I was again.

I found another gambling table, and at this one there
was a man preaching.

—Be wary, ye sinners, he said. —You may find riches
that slide through your hands like water, but the goodness
of your souls is something not worth trading away. It will
stay with you, should you nurture it, a constant treasure.
Here you stand gambling away your eternal souls with cards
and drink and whoring. This land of vice requires that we all
remember the words of Psalm 1. I see you men need a repeat-
ing of these words, and I will do so, for the sake of your souls.

'Blessed is the man that walketh not in the counsel of
the ungodly, nor standeth in the way of sinners, nor sitteth
in the seat of the scornful. But his delight is in the law of
the Lord; and in his law doth he meditate day and night.

And he shall be like a tree planted by the rivers of water, that bringeth forth his fruit in his season; his leaf also shall not wither; and whatsoever he doeth shall prosper. The ungodly are not so: but are like the chaff which the wind driveth away. Therefore the ungodly shall not stand in the judgment, nor sinners in the congregation of the righteous. For the Lord knoweth the way of the righteous: but the way of the ungodly shall perish.'

The other men and I howled in laughter.

From the shadows behind the table, a thin-waisted woman looked at me sideways, her head tilted just a bit. I felt as if she had never looked at anyone but me that way. Her long hair and her eyes were dark brown, almost black, and her skin was pale white. Her lips were dyed a deep red and curled up at the edges. She wore a long dress that traced the dirt around her. The bottom hem was marked with it. But her grace . . . her grace was something to be seen.

I walked after her. —You know what he did, my companion? You know what he did?

—I can't account for the deeds of no man, she said in a soft voice. —Can't barely account for my own.

I think it was then that she took my hand, or perhaps I took hers. But she led me to a house of three stories. Burning inside were the brightest lanterns. There was not a shadow to be found in any corner. And in the hall many men sat on chairs, with women all around them.

An older man in a suit walked up to us. —You're sure now? he asked me. —I have women of all kinds. From all over the world. You can travel the world through my women. You can have three continents in one night, if you're up to the task.

—You'll sell me the world, I said, and I thought it was with some cynicism.

But he replied without a trace of irony. —I will sell you the world in these walls.

The woman I was with flashed her dark eyes, and for a moment I saw the flash of Joanna's eyes. But Joanna was lost, far from me, farther still since what had happened in the alley. The woman shared hard words in a soft language with the man. French, it must have been. No language has ever been invented in which cursing sounds so beautiful. To match their beautiful, hard words, I uttered some of my own. I laughed as I cursed at the little man.

The woman pulled me away. Up a staircase we went. About halfway up the first flight, I heard a noise coming from behind us that made me turn. It was the lofty notes of a violin bow being pulled across strings. The melody was high and haunting, and I dragged the beautiful woman back down the stairs towards it.

A dwarf stood stock-still in the middle of the room as if nothing else existed, making a song as women in long skirts pulled men this way and that. The violin was almost the length of his torso. He played and played, and I watched, tears streaming down my face.

—If that's what you're looking for, just buy a ticket to a show. The woman laughed.

His bow dipped and dragged. The world moved around him, and his music moved, too.

The woman led me up the stairs, and he disappeared from my view, but still the music snaked through the air. I could hear it even when the woman had pushed me into one of the bedrooms down a long hall. I could hear it when she closed the door behind us.

The light in the room was low. There was a bed with grey cotton sheets on it, and they seemed soft, worn. I walked to an open window to feel air on my tear-stained cheeks. The spell of the alcohol had left me a bit, I was weak and susceptible, and something like the soft night breeze through a third-story window could destroy me.

She joined me at the window, then pressed her lips against mine and opened her mouth to kiss me in a way that my wife had not until after we had married. Certainly not like this, the first time our lips had met. But this woman was different, from a faraway place where women are different, I supposed, though she felt like any other woman has ever felt. Like the way my wife feels.

I moved back, and through some magic she loosened her dress in an instant. It fell to a soft pile on the floor, the light making it all wrinkles and shadows and soft pockets. She wore nothing under it, and there her body was, shining gold in the dim light, the hair under her arms and between her legs dark and curled. Her nipples were the color of wine. Her lips moved, and out of them came soft words that might well have been poetry. The edges of her lips curled up in a smile as if she was happy to be here with me. She stepped out of the center of the mound of cloth on the floor, and her gold skin moved towards me, her arms out and raised just a bit, stretching towards me.

Out the window I could hear the men at the gambling table in the street put up a roar. I could hear the voice of the preacher. —In the house of the Lord, ye shall stand revealed. Away will fall your worldly mask, and you will be naked as at birth, with all your deeds laid bare.

Her hands found me and pulled me closer, and those strained notes from the violin edged under the door, floating up to my ears. I rested my head on her shoulder, and I wept again, with the tears wracking my shoulders, making me hitch up against her. She supported me for some time, and as the tears did not subside, she laid me down on the bed and pressed herself on top of me.

I heard a voice coming in from outside, rivaling that of the preacher's.

O happy breast!
Nor care of courts, nor pride of birth,
Can ruffle thy smooth rest;
No scene of gilded riot
Disturbs thy star-lit quiet,
Nor dims thy dream of heaven with mists of earth—
O happy breast!

My body clenched in spasms of tears. She lay atop me like a raft on stormy water.

She brought her hand to the side of my face. —Some men need to cry more than they need other things. You ain't the first, and I imagine you won't be the last.

She soothed me and rubbed my face until I ceased crying.

—You'll have to pay all the same, she said.

—Of course, I said.

We stayed there, though she had rolled off me and was now at my side. —There was a fire not long ago, she said after a time of silence. —You could see it from that window here. One of the tents went up. All dancing orange. Then it lit up the other tents and some of the houses. The way they glow with light at all times, we couldn't tell at first. Just thought it was the light inside. Then it spread and spread, eating up a whole row of structures. There was people running and swarming. I wanted to walk into the streets and see it up close, but I had business to do. Men on sprees. Men jabberin' drunk and miserable and sad. Saw it all through that window. Twenty-three men died in the end. Those lights were something to see.

I could think of nothing to say. I had begun to drift through doors of my mind that had been opened too far by the terror of the night. Through doors opened even wider by the alcohol and her words.

—I killed a man once. Took the single life that had been given him. I was out in the trees and the dirt and the bushes, tracking a deer. It was quiet, so quiet, but I could sense something besides me and the deer there. Sometimes, out in the trees and the wild like that, you start developing the sense for things. Like when you know something growing is poison and you know to stay away. You become almost a part of that world, that brown and dirt and green and shadow. And I sensed it. Something besides me and the deer. But I couldn't see it or hear it none. Just knew, in some way, that we weren't alone.

—I came upon the deer. And I paused, I recall, because its head was down and its long neck looked so tender and gentle. Like grace, it looked like grace. Then I heard the softest noise in the bushes. So soft even that the deer didn't hear it. She just kept eating the green leaves and grass. I pictured the darkness in her mouth, like the way a cave is lightless, like the way the night sky would be lightless but for the stars.

—I turned real quick to the place I'd heard the noise. There was someone there, something wearing antlers on its head, though I knew right away it wasn't no deer. I saw a deep brown face, the slope of a nose, and the fullness of lips. So quiet this man was, but I was quieter. As he pointed an arrow at the neck of that deer, I turned my gun to him. Animal, man. I turned my gun. When I pulled the trigger, it was as if everything exploded. The leaves and the bush shook, and it was like the forest had combusted. All that shaking green. The deer was gone.

—I walked to the spot where I had aimed. An Indian lay there, dying, bleeding slow and fatal. He was speaking words I'd never understand. His blood was everywhere. I reloaded my rifle, and for a second his eyes met mine, then he looked down to the earth. Like that deer's neck, like grace. There was just the sound of the gun, and then everything was silent.

She worked her hands over me, above and under my clothes.

—I told my wife once before she married me. Told her

what I'd done, who the man she was marrying was. But she stopped me. We were sitting by a fire, and she put her hands over my eyes, and everything was dark and warm, like I imagine it is before you come into this world. And she said, *I see goodness*. And I was good, then I was, because every time something that wasn't good came my way, I thought of those hands between it and me. Even in my own mind, in my own past. Those hands creating a barrier.

The hands of the woman I was with kept working me. Tears streamed down my face again, but I was becoming aroused. I found a bottle beside the bed and drank from it and began to feel its glow. I felt her body under mine, twisting and moving, arousing me further. I ran my hands over her curves, grabbing handfuls of her skin. She went along with it, as if we were dancing and she knew all the moves I was making before I made them.

—You see? she said. —You see how it can be?

Maybe she said more, but though my body was working, I slipped outside myself. She lifted her hips and lowered the softness of herself over me, her back arching. Her hands kept moving like some sort of secret language. Her warm hands like a poultice, drawing the pain of the night out of me. She moved that way, and the pleasure was greater and greater until all of me had been drained away, and I lay there limp and listless.

When I awoke this morning, she was sleeping naked beside me. The music had ceased; the bustle from outside was still in the grey before dawn. I sat down to write, thinking, *By God. By God.*

My beloved,

It grows most dark. I am coming. I am coming.

Your husband

My dear,

Stephen is dead. It was his body that lay lifeless in the north. Father identified it despite the rot and the bloat death had caused. He returned a different man. Shaken. Perhaps broken.

Late at night, shadows fall across the floors. They slide and come closer. They retreat and fall back. They are coming. They extend from the tips of the branches of trees. They hide in the form of clouds crossing the moon. But they are something different entirely, a much more sinister shade of black. They are the absence of light, not mere shadow. And once they step forward from their hiding places, once they present themselves, there will be no going back to the way things were. It will become their world.

Mother is dying. I know this now. I cannot look upon her without seeing it. It is in the shadowed hollows of her cheeks. It is in the depths of blackness beneath her eyes. It is in the milkiness of her eyes that were once the blue of oceans. It is in the stink that surrounds her, ever so faint, like dead roses. I comfort myself that she will die before she sees the horror in store for this world. It is coming. It is coming.

My dear, I fear your death has arrived as well. I close my eyes, and I see it coming at you from the edge of a room, from the shadows of the saloon, from a darkened doorway. I see it coming in gun or knife or blunt object swinging through the air. I see Death spilling your precious blood, the blood pouring and expanding into a great pool that shimmers. I write these lines to a lifeless body. I write words to a ghost that haunts the places I once called my home. How I pray this is not true. How I fear it is.

The world is naught but shadows, death. The world is naught. It shakes as I look upon it. I try to still the shaking of my body, but it is not my body shaking; it is all I see. It trembles and disintegrates. There is nothing as it was.

My dear, please do not have fallen into the shadows and terror that torment me. Please be safe. Please help me find some way back. The path has turned midnight, and I am lost upon it.

With all my love,
Joanna

MARCH 2, 1849

The Indian found me a day outside of San Francisco. This time there were no feathers foretelling him. I did not come upon his trail. One moment the trees were filled with a hum, as if they had begun to come alive and were vibrating in their first stirrings. The hum rose, revealed itself as low singing. Then the Indian limped into view.

He looked worse than the last time I had seen him. His gait was unsteady, and it was like his skin was crawling away from him. An odor of rot, faint and sickening, hung about him like a cloak.

—You have been traveling with others. Were they others like you? His mouth cracked a black slit into his sick face as he spoke. —Tell me what you learned traveling with these men like you.

—That it's best traveling alone. If I could travel without my own self, I would do that.

He laughed as much as his withering frame would allow, but even that turned into coughs that wracked his shoulders. Finally, he righted himself and regained his composure. —Come, travel with me. I am almost dead, and it will be like traveling with no one at all.

As we walked, he scattered the gold behind us. He did it as if he could no longer be bothered about it. He did not stop to see what became of it, and, for my part, I walked on with little concern as well.

—Still, this burden stays heavy, he said. He showed me his pouch. It was full to the top with shining gold.

We walked and walked. We walked across a long, flat land with sandy ground and a ridge of rock far off in the distance. Our footsteps echoed a long way behind us. As the sun fell, the shadows of our legs and torsos lengthened. Always shining behind us was that gold. It winked up at the slipping sun, shining slow and lurid like some creature covered in ooze and slithering. It was almost profane, the way it glinted. It mingled and fell with the white feathers, and the white and the gold were like the colors of angels in ancient gilded Bibles, with rays of sun bursting out of the clouds to announce their arrival.

Late in the afternoon, the Indian fell to the ground, weeping. There he sat in a heap, his shoulders shaking.

I wanted to go to him and show him some sort of comfort, but I could not touch a man that sick. It occurred to me that I had not hesitated in letting the Companion touch me. He had been a different kind of sick, a kind of sick I should have worried more about being near.

Through his tears, the Indian talked. His voice was whispery, and I had to lean in to hear him.

—I had a life, he said. —I had friends and family, with

whom I cooked and played games and spoke late into the night. How many more times will I hunt? How many more times will I carry grain? How many more times will I wash my hair and my body? How many more stories will I tell? How many more times will I stay awake at a fireside until the sun breaches the sky, talking about the troubles and the joys of the world? How many more times will I wake up, wondering if it was a dream or a memory? It is over, over.

He hung his head and wept quietly. When he looked up, his tears were no longer falling. —Listen: this is my last story. Coyote will undo the world, just as he made it. Men will destroy much, that is true enough, but it was Coyote who made men. Who gave them hands like lizards that grasp and break. But I have seen how Coyote will undo things.

—Listen: there will be great things that men call riches that Coyote will make. He will make a giant pearl that rolls on the sandy floors of the ocean that the fish gods and Ho-ha'-pe, the mermaids, kick like a ball and use in play. One day they will fight over it, not because it is something men consider riches, but because there are rules to their play and someone will have violated them. A mermaid will cut off the head of a fish god, and his skull will slowly show as the water eats his scales away. And the skull will roll and swirl with the giant pearl. The lover of the fish god will walk alongside it, weeping, for years until the burden of her grief passes, then alone the skull and the pearl will roll on the floor of the ocean together. One day man will see it there, shining, and he will want it, as he wants all riches.

—While the tale of the pearl finishes in the seas,

Coyote will have made a great heart of gold and silver and the stones men think magic. He will hide it in the mountains somewhere across the seas in a land far beyond the land of my people or even your people. And there the cougar god of the mountain will think little of it. It will be a stone like any other stone. Sometimes the cougars will dig for it, sometimes they will let it lie, sometimes they will talk to it, and sometimes they will let it do the talking. But always the dull grey stones will be of as much value to them.

—Until one of the cougar gods decides to use the shine of its golden and silver parts as a mirror. He watches his face change in imperceptible degrees by days and weeks. He watches the sky in his forehead in the shine of the minerals. He watches and watches until one day his son tries to save him from his reflection. But the cougar god kills his son when he attempts to sneak away his prize, for he never lets it out of his sight. Maybe it is the son's blood or the reflection of the cougar's fire in the light of the heart that draws men, but that is when men see the heart.

—In the skies, there will be a bird. Not Kah'-kool, the raven, not Yel'-lo-kin, the bird who carries off the children, not We-pi-ah'-gah, the golden eagle. A great and terrible bird dripping with riches. Its bones will be stones that men covet, and its flesh will be precious to men—delicious to devour. The bird will fly over the lands so high that no man can see it. It will eat the clouds and the bugs and the air. The bird will know as much as Coyote knows, so Coyote, who loves his tricks, will make the things the bird eats fly low so it has to swoop down where men can see it. And of course, men will do what they always do to that which is majestic and alive. They will kill it.

—And deep in the earth will slither a great snake that grows from the poisons men who disrespect the earth bring. A snake with eyes of ruby, teeth of diamond, and venom not like poison but like an elixir. Whatever it bites grows and flourishes and becomes strong as an old tree with many rings. The snake will know little, but it will feel every footstep and every shovel and every dance for ancestors or the dead. It will slither and it will know, and Coyote won't have that, either. Instead of killing the snake outright, Coyote will make the center of the earth hot so the snake's blood begins to boil and it has to come closer to the surface of the earth. And then it can hide no more, and man will see it and say, *It is a monster! And I want its eyes!*

—So man (and of course they will be men who have pale faces, men who understand so little) will dive into the ocean with lungs he has made himself (for white men are stupid but clever in a way that is dangerous to all, in a way that manipulates to meet its own ends). So man will dive into the ocean, and man will delve into the mountains, and man will shoot into the sky and down into the earth. And when the pearl is found, when the heart is captured, when the bird is slain and the snake rooted from the earth, then the world will fall apart at the seams. For man, men like you, could never understand these things are linked to the corners of the earth, and when those corners are pulled, the earth collapses on itself. The world becomes a vortex that everything sinks into. And there Coyote will be, with his mouth open, waiting to close over all and swallow it into darkness.

—Then Coyote will be alone to roam the darkness. And perhaps he will vomit out the fish and the cougars and the birds and the snakes. But I pray and make requests that Coyote never vomit out the white man into any world he makes.

Here he said no more. His weeping had stopped, turned into a weak anger. A trace of fire was all that was there in his rage.

I looked around in the fading light. Already deep shadows were beginning to form. I stared into them. —I wonder what it will be like in that void.

—I hope your kind stays there forever.

I thought of how it would feel, lonely and cold, with nothingness too much to bear. And then I thought of the men I know, the men I had encountered, how vicious and cruel and foul they could be and often were. And I could think of no safer place for them. And if I, too, must be there, then at least the world was safe from them. From all of us.

—Come, now, I said finally. —We have some way to go.

The Indian stood, and behind us I could see the grass in the sandy soil had withered and yellowed and fell where we had stepped. It marked our path as clearly as the feathers did.

Night was about to fall, but we were coming near the ridge of rocks, and I wanted to camp there for the night, feeling it would provide some shelter. Howls sounded in the distance, and shelter became something that concerned me even more.

We reached the rock shelf in the last strains of light. We

climbed it, and it dropped off into a little alcove of rocks. Picking out steps carefully, we made our way down. I spotted something that looked like a table made out of rock, with rocks around it like chairs. Sitting up straight in one of the rocks was a figure.

—Hello? I called out.

There was no answer, but the closer we got to the base of the rock, the more I was sure it was a man. He sat with his back to us, but I saw his cotton shirt, his hat tilted back on his head, and one of his boots splayed off to the side.

—Sir?

The Indian held out a hand to stop me. —Something is wrong. I don't like this place.

—Maybe he's hard of hearing, I said, but I knew the Indian was right. Bad feelings echoed between those rocks like whispering voices.

—I am afraid, the Indian said.

We made our footfalls as soundless as dried leaves dropping from branches. We reached the bottom of the ledge and climbed to the flat-topped rock and the rocks around it. To the figure of the man. Just a few steps away, I called out again. But this time my voice was so soft it was barely a whisper. —Sir?

He did not turn towards us.

We came abreast of the man, and I realized he had not moved even once in all the time we'd been coming down. Shadows of dusk were creeping up at our sides, down the rocks, edging into the air all around us. The Indian had stopped, and I stood there alone. I took another step, and he immediately took two back.

When I got up close, the face I saw was as shrunken and leathered as a dried apple. The eyes were black holes, the meat of them probably eaten out by vicious birds some time back. The mouth was shut. He was too dried out to smell much anymore, but there were faint odors of rotten meat and lilacs past full bloom, withering on the vine.

—He ain't no danger to us, I said.

The Indian stepped closer, and we could see from the dried blood on the man's shirt that violence had been done to him. No knife or gun or criminal remained to tell the tale. We could only see the end of his story. Left sitting here as if at a gruesome supper table. Like a blind fortune-teller speaking no good fate for whoever came by.

Looking at his face, I thought I noticed a stirring. A glimmer of a motion at his mouth and along his jaw. But I knew it could not be; the light was failing, and in addition my eyes have not been the most reliable in the recent past. I put the idea out of my mind, but then I saw the same stirring. I stepped back, and the Indian did, too. I knew he had seen something as well.

—What—?

—Quiet.

The lower half of the dead man's face stirred unmistakably now, the mouth moving as if to form words. Cracks appeared in the brittle skin around the lips. What could this dead man have to say to us? Would he tell us his story or our own? I stood rooted to the spot, waiting for whatever words would come.

The mouth opened the slightest bit. Slowly, almost imperceptibly, it edged open more and more. Still no sound came. But something else did.

At first I thought it was a pale white tongue reaching out in a poor attempt to wet those cracked lips. It certainly moved just like that, the end flickering up to the top lip first, then at the lower one. But the thing coming out of the mouth kept extending, falling down the chin under its own weight. It was a white worm.

It dropped to the chest of the dead man and slithered on the cotton of his shirt. As I stared down at it, more worms, smaller ones, joined it. And something shining. Something that looked like gold. Soon the worms and more gold pieces covered the dead man's chest and lap.

I turned away in disgust. The Indian had done the same. Perhaps death was too close a notion for him to keep looking upon that husk of a man.

The Indian and I left the alcove of rocks. We walked in the darkness, and the howling coming from far off didn't disturb me as it had, even when we set up our camp out in the open. And even here in the open, I can still almost smell the way the rocks held in that old death. It has clung to me and can't be shaken off.

MARCH 3, 1849

I dreamt last night of an enormous beast. It opened its jaws on green fields, swallowing them, making the earth shake and crumble. Thick trees, tall and ancient, snapped like seedlings when they met the rock of its shining teeth. Its guts worked like the gears of mill engines, grinding and clattering all at once. Its eyes were the emptiest things you could imagine. Like the black of starless space, they were, with the sheen that comes to a man's eyes in the moment death takes him.

The beast wasn't alive, yet it acted like something living. Something that had to be fed. Nothing could fill up the beast. It just kept chewing and spitting and taking, growing all the while, becoming bigger than any man or even the earth itself. And it wasn't just the earth it ate. After the earth was gone, it began to feed on men, even men who fed it everything around them. Soon there was nothing but this beast, this machine that grows and consumes. What will happen when it's got nothing left to feed on? I wondered. Will it feed on itself? The dream didn't get that far, but I fear that one day I will dream it all the way to the end and see ruin as I have never seen ruin before.

Maybe I had this dream because of the Indian's story about his Coyote. But this beast was something different. The Indian says his Coyote created at one point, and this beast could never create anything. This beast can only destroy.

I awoke from my dream sweating, hearing howls way off somewhere. It was night. The fire had died. My heart was beating as if it were something wild that had been captured.

MARCH 4, 1849

We are now traveling largely to the east, and gold country is right upon us. All around are men prospecting and mining, swirling water and throwing dirt up in the air, blowing on it to see what flies away and what falls. There are shouts of gold at every turn and camps full of men making more in a day than they had in a month where they came from. I wove in and out of these camps while the Indian hung back or hid in the trees. He was nothing to fear any longer, he tells me, but he will be damned if he can stand the smell of that many white men.

The Indian was preparing to disappear into the blue oaks when we found another camp. We smelled smoke and stepped into a beautiful clearing. The trees were stronger and bigger here. Flags of red and yellow and green, dyed so strongly that they were like lights against the grey sky, flew between the white trees. They snapped in the breeze coming up out of the west, carrying in from the ocean.

The Indian paused at my side. —This is not a white man's camp.

I knew he was right.

With the Indian at my side, I walked closer to the flying flags. There was a stillness quite like the one in the stone ridge a couple of days ago, and I realized that the only sound in the camp was the whipping of those flags. The breeze had picked up. It was as if it had done so just to make the flags fly. At least, that was the thought in this mind that I no longer seem able to account for.

We called out hellos in Spanish. Our footfalls were heavy sounding on the dry ground as we approached. The fire had ceased to crackle. It was but embers, glowing red and white, flaring here and there in bursts where some dry twig shifted in the wind and came close to them. The camp was deserted.

—Where do you think these men have gone? I asked the Indian. —They seem to have left in a hurry and have been gone some time.

The Indian nodded.

I was having a hard time looking at his face, scabrous as it had become. I had never known a man could appear so defiled. But right then, I didn't have much time to think about his face.

—I don't like this. He walked around the camp, around the colorful flaring flags and the tents. —The earth is disturbed by the hooves of horses and by many feet. They head in many directions, but mostly they head this way. He gestured off through the trees, off to the north. He smiled, and on that melting-away face, the smile was something horrible to behold. —Would a white man like you care to see what's become of them?

Without any assent from me, we began in the direction the Indian had pointed. The tracks in the dirt and the grass and the underbrush were hard to miss. Many men had ridden and run that way as if devils were chasing them.

I thought I had grown accustomed to coming upon horrors. This new world forming seems to hold nothing but them for me. And yet when we came upon that first long pole sticking up from the ground, when we saw what sat grimly atop it, I caught my breath deep inside me. The head on that pole was swollen from the batterings it had taken, the eyes little more than slits. The brown color of the skin was purple and navy blue with bruises, with dried blood, and with the flies the blood had attracted. They buzzed with a cruelty innocent of itself. They did not think, so how could they know their swarming and buzzing was a further insult to this already defiled piece of man?

There was blood all around. Trees bloody. Little golden wildflowers covered in blood. Stalks of grass trampled and maroon and dripping. The dirt on the ground moist with blood.

The head had something stuffed into its mouth. It looked like a hairy apricot, but it was too large and hairy. My breath caught again when I realized it was a dried human scalp. For some reason this last sight made the bile rise, and I had to lean aside to vomit.

The Indian walked around, his ruined face betraying nothing of what he thought. —A battle was fought here. If a battle is when one destroys another by surprise, without a chance, as if it is their right to do as they please, to whomever

they please. But to white men, that is what a battle is. Their
will is the only right. Without a second thought. The men
who did this are probably singing songs somewhere by now.

I wandered around and began to realize that the spot
must have once been a camp of its own. There were pits dug
not far away filled with feces and urine that stank. I looked
down into them and saw bodies lying there. I vomited again,
this time further desecrating the bodies with my bile.

The Indian stood with me then, and for a moment I
thought he would push me down into the pit. His eyes were
hard, the only part of him left that could show anything,
though they, too, were dimmer than they had once been.

—This is the work men like you do, he said. —This is
what you have brought with you. Your coming has brought
death, ruin, shit, piss, blood, fear, death, death. If only you
all had died in the coming from the East. If only the spirits had taken your breath as you slept, if only the sun had
baked your heads, if only the rains had drowned you. If
only, far back in the land where you came from, your mothers
had murdered you as you cried newborn cries.

I felt dangerously close to the edge of the latrine pit and
dangerously close to him. There was nowhere for me to step
that was safe. —And yet you are traveling with me. Why?

The Indian took a deep breath, and his small frame
seemed to rise and fill with it, growing just a bit. He glanced
down at the pit, at the bodies. When he looked at me, his
eyes were moist. Water leaked from one but was sucked
right into the dried cracks of his diseased face. —That
remains to be seen.

We walked slowly away from the ruin and back to the camp with the bright flags. Though it seemed disrespectful, we went through the tents, looking for supplies. Everything had been taken already.

Later I was passing through a camp of mostly white men that the Indian stayed away from and heard tell of what had happened. A group of white miners had taken quarrel with a group of Mexicans. They had ridden through this latter camp messy with the Mexicans' blood and heavy with their possessions, which had among them not a small amount of gold. The men related the story as if it was just the news of the day, which I suppose to them it was.

MARCH 5, 1849

Again and again, I use the word "horror." A shock and a shudder, something deep and repulsive. Horror, horrid, horrify, horrific, horrible. There is something jagged about it that drives deep like a splinter of wood festering and swelling the skin around it. It heats and chills like a fever; it ripples over the surface of the mind. The swelling and intensity burn up the spine, into the skull where they settle and simmer after the shock of impact. And somewhere in that impact is "terror"—in the windlessness of it, the dull strike it makes against you.

I once saw a man said to have the horrors, who came drinking every day, then came no more. On the third day he didn't show up at the saloon, I went to his rooms to make sure he hadn't fallen dead with nobody to find him. He was lying in his bed. His hands shook, and his arms and legs moved like snakes. When he saw me, he asked me to lean close to him. I did so haltingly; I thought perhaps he would bite me or undertake some other violent act. But all he did was whisper what was going on in his tortured mind.

—A beast on a wide, flat plain, he said, —its eyes burn, it is coming, it is coming, it burns, it retches, it smells, beast horror east, the way it moves like water in a storm, beast burning in the night, the sky its eyes, tearing and terrorizing, beating beast, moaning monster, pride, gain, love of pain, the pain is mine and it's at once, the flat plain pain moves and dances and the grasses trampled, the eyes like diamonds, diamond spit, ruby drool, the night a fire, fire eyed, beast eat east beasty, beasty beast on fire, the night.

The horrors, he had. I have always wondered what that man saw, drying out and shaking as he was.

Still. "Horror" does not match up to any of it. I wonder if there could ever be a word that does.

MARCH 6, 1849

I force my mind to you, though I do not deserve your comfort. I remember you on a night when you wept. —Children, you said, your frame curled up in our bed, shaking softly. It seems to me that everything you do is soft. —Children, you said again. —Why has the Lord not blessed us with children? You wondered if it was the fault of your body or perhaps something you had done. A penance. I could not stand for such talk, thinking of your goodness.

—What would become of children out here? I asked you. —Would they learn from the missionaries how to cheat the Indians? Would they play in the saloon, running among the guns and the glasses of whisky? Would they lose their lives to bears or have coyotes carry them off? Would we raise them only to lose them to war or battles fought for God knows what? It's better, Joanna. Children are fragile, and this world we live in is not an easy one.

Still you wept. There was no consoling I could do, nothing I could say to change it. And though I did not say it, I thought again and again, *If it's anyone's sin, it must be mine.*

Those dark days in the woods and the brush swell now. My actions in San Francisco. That woman I took ill-gotten comfort in. I try to quell them with thoughts of you, thoughts of beloved Joanna. But I know I do not deserve the comfort you bring.

MARCH 7, 1849

The Indian disappeared, though I know he is not far. His journey and mine are close to finished, and our paths remain tightly bound up in one another. But today for a while, he was gone as if lifted gently on the bay breeze and carried off. Not a feather remained.

I came across a camp of four men. Three of them wore felt hats that sagged down at the brims. Their clothes were patched at the knees and elbows, and it seemed they had been scrubbed until the cloth gave up all the dirt it had accumulated and some of the color. The other man wore brown leather, and it was beginning to wear into lighter tan in some spots.

It was about lunchtime, and they seemed to be settling back into their camp to eat after a morning of mining. The youngest man, with a face that could barely grow whiskers, was at the fire, stirring and preparing food. His movements around the pots were graceful. It seemed as if he knew exactly where he stood with the task at hand. Yet there was something about his face. Something that looked mournful, as if he had lost a love.

—May I join you men for lunch? I called. —I have coins that I can pass along to you, if need be, to pay some.

The man in leather sized me up. Then he laughed, a gravely, mirthless laugh. —Your coins are useless, friend. We're pulling in more gold than we rightly know what to do with. We have food enough, I suppose, to share with you at the moment, but don't get any ideas about joining us here at our claims.

—Of course not, sir, I said. —Just looking for something to fill my stomach besides berries.

As I came near the fire, the young boy looked up at me. There was something of a longing and a pleading there. I did not know what to make of that expression, so I turned away.

Something hit the ground, and the young man flinched as if he were a horse shying. I looked over and saw the man in leather cocking his arm, ready to throw another rock at the young man.

—We leave you alone all morning, and the food ain't even ready when we come back? he said, scowling. —What have you been doing here? God knows you aren't pullin' in gold or really doing much to help our cause. It's a wonder we keep you along. As it is, your share of what we got is going down all the time. Seems you can't even do the chores of hearth for anything. Damned if I know what you're good for.

—I spent the morning cleaning from breakfast, the young boy said. A shrillness had come into his voice. — And mending clothes and watering the horses and fixing and cleaning up the tents and making the camp presentable.

You all act as if you can throw things about and they will go back to their places by magic. There ain't no magic here, just me picking up after you. And if lunch is late, I truly am sorry, but it will be ready soon, and then you can go back to prospecting and leave me here to work in peace.

One of the men in a felt hat was unlacing his cotton shirt near the neck. He pulled it over his head, revealing a taut stomach and a chest of small muscles. He crumpled the shirt into a ball and threw it with some venom the young boy's way. —Damn lot of lip from someone who ain't bringin' in any gold. You can get sewing this after you finish our lunch. And I don't want any of them sloppy stitches that fall out in a few days' time. I want you doing it right so I don't have to wait for your slow self to do it for me again.

The young boy picked up the shirt off the ground and folded it neatly. Then he carried it over to a board lying across two rocks like a table and set it down.

I felt uncomfortable watching the whole thing. It was a relief when lunch was served and the men were occupied with it. They were mostly quiet, shoveling in their food.

Then the man in leather spoke. —I believe I would like a song to go with my lunch. Boy, why don't you favor us with a song? It will help me to digest, I think.

The other men, except for the youngest, glanced at each other, smirking, as if a good joke had just been told.

A resigned look came over the youngest man's face as he put his plate down. He began to sing a mournful song.

One of the other men stopped him. —I ain't in the mood for crying songs, boy. You know what we want you to sing.

The young boy stood up. He took a deep breath, but nonetheless his voice came out thin and sad.

> *If she makes a scolding wife*
> *As sure as she was born,*
> *I'll tote her down to Georgia*
> *and trade her off for corn.*

The men around the campfire howled, slapping their thighs.

The youngest man sat down and resumed eating without saying a word.

Lunch was finished then, and the men dumped their plates near the feet of the youngest man. His eyes flashed as if he was about to say something. But in the end he said nothing and looked down.

—Now I want all this sewing and cleaning and washing done and dinner ready by the time we get back, hear? the man in leather said to the youngest boy. —We're working hard out there, and we deserve some comforts when we come back. Things are real pretty for you now, sitting here all day and reaping our rewards, but that's going to change a sight if you don't start making this a comfortable place for us.

The man in leather turned to me. —Normally, I'd ask you to help, but as you can see, we have our homemaker here. Wouldn't want to take no work away from her.

With that, the men trooped off, back to their work.

As soon as they were gone the youngest man looked up. He closed his eyes for a second, then stared down at the ground. Finally, he looked up again and gazed into my eyes.

—You're not the kind of man who would behave this way, are you? Behave like a brute?

—I don't suppose I am, I said hesitantly. —Then I also don't appear the kind of man who would stop such behavior when I see it.

—A good man can't always force the good inside himself out on other men, he said. His eyes were warming with every word, becoming less shy and flitting.

—I don't know that I am what you would call a good man.

—Oh, don't say that. For I know it ain't true. I can tell a good man when I see one. A man who wouldn't treat me this way. A man who might take one of those there horses and ride me off and take me away from all this. I thought of going myself, you see, but I don't know if I could make it out there alone. But a man like you could help me and protect me. I just know you could.

—What are you saying? I asked.

He grabbed my arm, and the pleading in his eyes became something as bright and dancing as the fire near us. —Take me away. Please take me away. I can cook and I can clean and I can sew. I can make you happy and relaxed, I promise you. I can do for you all the things you need done. You won't never have to worry yourself. But please say you'll take me away.

I tore away from him, leaving his big eyes pleading at me. I stepped back without a word, trying not to see how pitiful he looked.

He reached out towards me, his hands finding my waist. —Other things, too. I know how to make a man happy in so many ways. I could make you feel so good, a good man like you.

I tore away the hands grabbing my belt and pushed him off. He fell to the ground and began to weep. I left him there, crying at the campfire.

—You're like all the rest, he spat at me. —Just like all the rest.

MARCH 8, 1849

My thoughts have been in torment for some time. Each step drives me deeper into myself as I wonder what kind of man I have become. The youngest man's final words stay with me: *You're like all the rest.* And I hear the Indian's words about white men, men like me who have crossed the plains, who have taken boats here, and what they have brought with them. Who am I, and where do I stand? I wish I could sort through this question. It seems as much a mystery to me as the Indian's feathers once seemed. I have long been someone who watched, who did not take part in the often senseless, sometimes brutal nature of the world. But I, like every man, am leaving a mark. If I were to die now, I would not like this mark as it stands.

As these dark thoughts marched through my head, my feet moved over lush ground. Moss and lichen shaded the earth many colors of green, and trees reached into the sky, their tops waving casually against the blue. Mushrooms sprang in the cool fecundity of the growing earth. Every now and then, my boots crushed one into a spot of slickness, and my footing slipped. But never did I fall, and I felt that, if I did, the soft ground would cushion me like a pillow.

The sun crept out from behind the edge of a cloud and made its way down to me through a filter of green leaves, playing about the earth, reaching the few wildflowers that had managed to spring up. I emerged from my thoughts a bit, remembering the world I had found away from the saloon, away from the angry men and the occasional killing that came out of this anger, the world I had lingered in long before Joanna. Though it had been harsh and dark, it had sometimes pulled back a kind of veil and revealed a quiet beauty. A wide openness and a breathless space, something empty and full at once, resounding. A world of the natural.

A world that later Joanna and I walked through, talking to one another of our minds, of the dreams we had the night before, of the things I would not have wasted words on if I was with another besides my dear wife. My dear wife. As I thought of her now, I reflected on all I must tell her of my journey, and my mind grew black once again. Would she reject me? Wouldn't it be right for her to do so? Could even I accept the man I was?

Yet the earth around me remained in beauty, untroubled by my fate or what had become of me since I had stepped out of my home.

A starling flew through the low branches and came to rest on one. It almost seemed to be looking down on me as it sang, trying to draw me out of myself. My mind started softening again, for I imagined it talking to me. The lilt of its voice asking me questions. *How are you so far away, so deep inside yourself, when all of this is around you? Hasn't this showing of the land always been able to calm your mind? What more could you want of this Western world? Why don't you look about you?*

I stood there listening to its song and the questions in it, and then I heard the sound of water running. I was overwhelmed with a sudden desire to sit by the banks of whatever stream it was, to cool my head and my mind in its waters, to strip off my clothes and submerge myself in it. I wanted to feel healed, I suppose. I wanted the flowing water in this growing place to wash my troubles from me. To make me feel some kind of peace could be had. Of course, I knew it would be mostly an illusion. But illusion was something I was willing to accept if it could provide me a moment's respite.

The thoughts of the water calmed me, and I walked through the trees breathing in the smell of the fertile loam. The sounds of the water grew, their dips and journeys over the rocks like a song themselves. The rushing water was powerful; I could tell that even from where I stood.

Now, as I write, I laugh to myself in a mirthless way. How could I have expected anything but ruin?

The gleam of the metal reached my eyes before anything else. It was turning and spinning in the sun, winking back up at it in an almost lascivious way. Lurid as a drunkard's advances. Gleaming, drawing attention to itself.

I stepped towards it as if towards a revelation. As the people native to this land must have felt ages ago coming upon a natural wonder that no one had ever seen before, that had never been described or spoken about. But this was the kind of wonder that was being offered now that people wanted to harness the world instead of live in harmony with it.

In the channel of water, metal cylinders turned, carrying water between the slats of their gleaming bars. Alongside the cylinders were wheels, and about the wheels were chains. Men pushed boxes on wheels alongside the edge of the water. Men turned wheels with handles on them. There were wheels and metal pipes and towers. The effect of all these grinding wheels and all these men working them was that a world of water had become a world of machine.

It seemed the men who had built this monstrosity existed now only to tend to it, to make sure its turning never ceased. To see that some wealth and power could be derived from these banks that I had longed to sink into and feel myself washed away by. No one in the water appeared to be doing anything like that. They were turning and grunting and taking what they could out of that water.

I turned back to the trees, but they no longer held even a semblance of peace for me. All I could hear was the turning of the wheels. I wondered how I had not heard it before.

The Indian found me some time later. We are not far now from the place he is headed, and that is not far from where I must leave him, strike north, and see if there is any room left for a man like me in the heart of my beloved.

—You are deep inside something, the Indian said to me.

—Or it is deep inside me, I replied.

—And we are coming upon something even deeper.

He showed me his buckskin bag. It was still full to the brim.

MARCH 9, 1849

The air has changed. The coolness of the winter has just begun to warm, and the ocean breeze has dried up like a thing left too long in the sun. The weight of my pack seems heavy but not as heavy as the gun I carry by my side. It has become a weight strapped to me. Its metal burns warm in the sun.

—Can you feel it in the ground? the Indian asked.

—Not in the ground, no. But in other places.

—It is coming. I hope you have decided on yourself. To hesitate now could be to lose all.

I did not question his vagueness, for I expected no clearer answer. He spoke less and less as we walked on. He sang songs deep in his throat, perhaps hymns to his Coyote asking for benevolence. Or, at the very least, an end to his tricks.

MARCH 10, 1849

I could not help but feel the rumbling. It was as if a massive storm had fallen from the sky and taken up its business with the earth. I lowered myself to the ground and pressed my ear against it. The sound of many hoofbeats echoed through it. It was as if the earth had many hearts, and all were beating at a feverish pace.

—Something's coming, I told the Indian.

—It has been coming for some time, he said. He seemed resigned to face whatever would come. I suppose he was no longer worried about death, and that took away other fears. For myself, I could not say the same.

In the distance, a cloud of dust rose across a dry grassland through which we had spent the morning passing. Forms emerged from this dust, men up high on horses, driving them as far and fast as they could. We watched them approach in slow motion. It would take some time before they reached us, yet it seemed it would take longer than that for us to find shelter away from the plain in a band of trees.

—What will we do? I asked the Indian.

—I will die; that much is clear, he said.

—What will I do?

—The answer to that has never been clear to me, he said.

I measured the distance between the wild riders and us once again. It would certainly be close, but there seemed a glimmer of hope in running for the trees. More hope, at least, than staying here in the open.

—Come! I shouted at the Indian and began to run.

My pack banged against my back and my gun against my side. My boots went up and down, and my heels slid painfully against the leather. Soon my breath was jagged. I tried to hold it for several strides, but it ripped out of me with each step.

The Indian was having a harder time than me, gasping about the pain he felt in his wasted body. —Stop, stop, please for a moment.

I could not continue on at that pace myself, and we stopped, gasping for air, doubled over our knees. We seemed to have gone nowhere, and the riders seemed to have advanced. They were still too far away to tell who they were, but I felt quite sure we had seen their work. We rested for a moment before I insisted we run again.

It went on like that, us running in starts and fits, and the riders coming ever closer. We had been glancing back so much that I stopped noticing what was ahead of us. When I finally looked at our destination, what I saw disconcerted me greatly.

A figure moved around at the edge of the trees. At first he seemed to be circling like a dog or a wolf, but then the

figure straightened out and headed for us. I was sure whoever it was could not help but see the riders coming our way.
The figure must have had a more pressing purpose, then.

We had no choice. We continued towards the trees and
the figure. And as we did, a certainty began to grow in me.
A certainty that the trail had run its course, and there was
fate at the end.

By the time I knew the figure was the Stranger, we had
slowed. The riders were not far, and in the dust we could see
that they were a group of men pushing and straining across
the plain. But it didn't matter, for the Stranger would reach
us first. We headed towards him with a deliberate walk.
There was no need in rushing anymore.

—Who the hell are you? he called out to me. —Traveling with that Injun thief? Make yourself known and declare
yourself, or you will have the same damn fate he'll meet at
the end of my gun and knife.

I turned towards the Indian. He stopped behind me.
He did not reach for a weapon to defend himself. He did
not reach for the bag of gold. He looked sure and defiant
in a way I thought the late stage of his sickness had completely taken from him. The feathers were falling fast, and
then they gathered around his feet and stopped falling
altogether. I did not see any left tangled in his hair. They
had all finally reached the ground.

—I am neither friend nor foe, I said.

—Oh no, the Stranger insisted. He drew his gun from
his belt and held it out before him. It had a long barrel and
a dark wooden handle, and I knew it to be the kind of gun

that could blow a hole straight through a man.

—No, no, he said. —There ain't no such thing no more as neutral. Any man can see this is war. You're with or you're against. There ain't nothing else, and there's no time to waste with refusing to declare yourself.

He strode closer, spit flying from his mouth and escaping the space between his gold teeth. For a moment, the sun caught my eye, and it seemed there were spaces in him, great gaps at the joints where his arms met his hands, where his elbows and knees were. His jaw opened, and a gaping emptiness was at the hinge of it.

I hesitated with my hand on my gun, waited until my vision lost its haze. My sight cleared, though he was no less fearsome. I focused on my gun. I had never shot it. I did not know its weight, its heft, its aim, all the things vital to shooting to kill. I would likely be committing suicide by trying to do so now.

I turned towards the Indian, who was still a few steps behind me. He had said himself that he was going to die. Would it make any kind of sense for me to die, too? His burden was not my burden; my only stake in anything was getting along my path. Getting to where my sweet wife struggled with the changing, shifting world. There was horror for her, I knew, and didn't I owe it to her to protect her from such? Hadn't I vowed to do so? My commitment to her was far greater than any commitment I had to some Indian who had wandered into my saloon.

I looked at the Stranger advancing. He had death in his eyes.

I pulled my gun from my belt and held it before me, pointing it at him. —There ain't no use coming up on us like that. Why don't you just put that gun down and—

—Declare yourself, he shouted. His face twisted in rage, and he seemed to be growing, increasing in size with every hard step.

I began to shake. —I got no allegiances, I cried. —I have no stake in any of this, don't you see?

My whole body shook. He could see it, and this only seemed to strengthen him, to make his outthrust pistol steadier and truer. Any moment, the choice would be made for me.

I took one look back at the Indian. As I faced the Stranger, my thumb was already cocking the hammer of my gun. The trigger slid down, released. It wasn't any accident.

The bullet entered the Stranger's head just left of his nose, destroying it as it went. He fell to the ground with a hole in his face and blood pumping out of it. The blood rushed down over his mouth. As he lay on his back, the blood came between the glittering shimmer of his gold teeth and the light of the sun.

The tattoo of the hoofbeats was gaining in sound and speed. The riders were upon us, and I could see them through the rising dust. On their faces were not the looks of conquest and destruction I had expected but looks of abject terror. They were running away from something.

One pulled up almost even with us when his face fell into a blank expression. He crumpled over the saddle of his horse. The horse kept on as if nothing had happened, and

the man slid slowly and liquidly over the side of the saddle, down and around until he was being dragged along,
the horse's hooves kicking at and jerking him. An arrow
protruded from his back.

The riders were being overtaken. All around me, they
fell. Others on horses circled them. I still could not make
out the others through the dust. I could only see arrows flying, knives flashing. I watched faces exploding, heads splitting open. Then the dust was about us, the riders were near
on top of us, and in the center of it all the dust cleared, and
I saw the other set of riders, the ones hunting down the
white men.

They were something to behold. Their skin shone in different shades from the colors of mahogany to honey. Their
long hair flew around them like banners snapping in the
wind. Their faces, though they were set and serious, were
beautiful, with wide-lipped mouths and intelligent, flashing
eyes. They carried knives and bows, and a few of them had
guns. But these fierce women were only part of the battalion
that was surrounding us.

A woman with one leg and a man with one arm worked
together to ride a horse and use weapons. The woman got
off the horse gracefully and went hand-to-hand fighting
with a somewhat injured man. She swung and maneuvered
as if the lack of a leg were a blessing. Before long the man
lay bleeding on the ground.

For a moment, I thought the man calling orders was
part of the group of white men who had been in flight. He
was young, and his features were fine. Then he swept back a

hand and off came his hat, and his auburn hair rolled down to his chest, at which I now saw a swelling. I looked harder, trying to see if it was *her*, the woman I had last seen lying in the dirt on that horrid San Francisco night. It might have been.

It wasn't long before the group had made their work of the white men. The dust began to settle as they pulled their horses around and circled back, making sure none of the men were left.

All about me lay corpses. Men with holes in them and missing parts that were strewn about like a child's playthings. Many of their horses headed for the trees, free to roam and graze. I looked for the Indian, but I did not see him. Then I noticed a crumpled form on the ground.

Instinctively, I knelt to help. His eyes were shut, and low cries escaped his mouth. There were no marks anywhere upon him other than the ones that the disease had made, but there didn't have to be at this late stage. The Indian had reached the end of his journey. I didn't think of his disease as I rested his head in my lap, cradling it. I thought only that a man was dying, a man who had done no wrong to me, and his dying needed to be eased. I did owe him that.

The woman who had been clad as a man approached us slowly. She towered above us in grace and regality. As if she had been born on horseback. Her auburn hair whipped across her face, hiding her hard eyes for a moment. She pointed her gun directly at my face. —State your intentions with that man.

—I didn't ride in with those other men, I told her. My eyes could not stray from the deep black hole at the end of the gun barrel.

—I know that. You would be dead if you had. Your intentions.

I considered all the things that could be called intentions. To live my life with some degree of peace and familiarity. To find my wife and to offer her succor. To press back the past and the wrongdoings. To find a place that was untouched, that would stay stable and not shift, that would be at odds with the rest of the running-away world. But in that moment, none of those things were my intention. — All I intend to do is sit here and aid this man in his passing. If you will let me do that, I am thereafter yours to do with what you will.

The gun lowered just a bit. The auburn-haired woman looked down at the Indian. She spoke a few words I could not understand.

The Indian opened his eyes and replied in the same language, his native tongue. His stream of words was long. It rose and fell and at times was drowned out completely by his moans of pain.

When he fell silent, the auburn-haired woman called out to someone behind her.

The red-haired woman with one leg hobbled into sight, a wooden crutch bearing half her weight.

—Clem, see this man onto your horse, and see that he don't get any ideas of running off.

Clem led me at gunpoint to the horse she had descended from. The man who had been on the horse with her was gone, riding with someone else. She motioned to it.

—Don't get any ideas, she said as I climbed up. —I've used this gun before on men just like you, and I don't have no fear of using it again.

When I was seated comfortably, I reached down to help her up.

But she looked scornful as she refused my hand and swung into that saddle more gracefully than I had. Her body pressed against mine from the back. The gun pressed into the small of my back.

The woman with auburn hair helped the Indian to his feet. It was a slow and painful process, one that elicited more than one cry of pain from him.

The others who had fought and defeated the men on horseback were coming around now, having hunted down the last of their enemies. They were mostly Indian and Mexican women. There were fierce-looking Celestial women, and every now and then a black woman, too. Not a few of the women's bodies were missing some piece—an arm, a leg, a hand—though the lack did not seem to bother them. All their faces were hard and without mirth, but no one looked cruel. It was as if they had an inevitable job to do, and now it was done. They paid little attention to the bodies all around us.

—Levi, why has this one survived? an Indian woman said, pointing at me.

The auburn-haired woman responded to her in the same tongue in which she had spoken to the Indian.

The group busied themselves adjusting their saddles and soothing their horses, who were still keyed up from the battle. A few of the women appeared to be discussing, then one with black hair and brown skin called out, and they all set off at a trot.

Clem kicked the horse we rode on with her one good leg, and we started off, too.

—Where are we going? I asked, but she did not answer me.

We rode and we rode. We rode past camps and across streams. We rode through trees and over meadows. It would have been a blessing that I was riding for once instead of walking, but I had no idea of what fate was in store for me. These women had not killed their enemies cruelly, but they had killed them all the same. And I certainly didn't appear too different from their enemies.

By nighttime, I was falling asleep in the saddle. The Indian's moans of pain kept rising above the beat of the horses' hooves. We crossed a stream in the darkness, then stopped at a village. Smoke billowed out of the grass-thatched roofs of the little houses that resembled beehives. Women came outside to greet us. They were mostly shorter than the women I rode in with and wore deerskin skirts. Several had thin lines tattooed down their faces.

I was led down off the horse and into one of the huts. Clem set about building a fire from the stack of wood along one side of the circular wall. There was a deerskin blanket on the floor on top of a grass mat.

—You may as well sleep, she said. —You don't know what tomorrow will bring for you.

—Do you know? I asked.

She said nothing, just kept at the fire.

—With all respect, ma'am, I can't die this way.

I expected a sneer to crawl across her features, but instead she turned to regard me in the dancing light from the beginning blaze. —How do you mean?

—I've made a choice, I said. —And if I were to die now, that choice would go unfulfilled. And I can't have that.

Her face grew hard. —We are not cruel people, so I won't punish your words. The fire sprang up, casting her face in a sinister light. —But I will be damned if I let a man like you tell me what will and won't be.

With that, she exited the hut, her wooden crutch hitting the ground hard with each step.

The woman who had called out and led us off earlier stood in front of the hut that night, I suppose so I wouldn't escape. Her hair flew like the wings of a raven in the wind. When the other women passed, they called her Maria. In the late hours of the night, she sang songs in Spanish. They were songs of love and faith and the fierceness those things could bring.

When she finished, I asked her, —Where is the Indian man who rode in with us? How is he faring?

—He is close to dead, Maria replied as if it was all the same to her one way or the other. —Do you hear them singing for him?

I heard them then. Low and high voices, in what seemed to be many languages. But those languages did not clash and spar with one another. Rather, they seemed to blend, to create one continuous stream of words and sounds. I listened for some time.

—What is this place? I asked after a while. Through the door of the hut, I watched fires dancing in other huts. They were like stars in a dark sky.

—The native women let us live here, she said. —They lived here with their kind, but one day, they were away gathering, and they came back to find there had been a slaughter. Their men, their children, the women who had been left behind were all dead. Men like you did it. But you knew that, didn't you? It's always men like you, coming from far away, seeking riches, and bringing death in exchange for them.

—I met the men like you one night, she said, —men who'd come West. One night howling with blackness and pain. And after that night, a part of me went back where I'd come from, and a part of me went on. And now I'm here, watching you and telling myself there's some reason you're still here. But a part of me is just waiting for your first wrong move.

I looked to the blackness on which she stood. No moon lit the ground, and there was no shadow. Something in me caught and hitched. I went inside. I lay down on the deerskin, but sleep would not come.

I drifted off eventually, for some time around dawn I awoke to the sound of footsteps. I barely had time to sit upright before Levi was standing in the hut.

—Get up, she said. —Come along.

—The Indian man we came in with, I said as we walked out the door. —How is he?

—Dead, she replied.

I stopped. —I had a right to be with him.

—Right? she said, whirling around. She had done herself up in the dress of a man, but the fire in her eyes had all the anger and righteousness that women are entitled to. —A man like you speaks of right? What would you know about right?

We stood there in the open space between the little houses, and around us the women watched. Levi's face kept shifting. Her features rode a line between man and woman, woman and man. At times I was not rightly able to tell who or what I was talking to. I looked down, and perhaps the sun was too high, but I could see no shadow beneath her.

—I traveled with him, I said. —I walked the same path he did, and it was my right to help ease his passing. To be there with him.

—Did you offer to carry his burden? The burden that, by all rights, should have been yours, not his? His burden carries the curse of your kind. It carries with it destruction, and it never left him. Did you once offer to ease that burden from him and let him live the few days he had left free of it?

I stepped back from the heat of her fury. She had not drawn her gun, but she might as well have. I felt like something deadly was pointed at me once again. My gaze fell from her to the ground.

—People soothed him along his way, she said finally, her anger fading a bit. —They did so better than you could have. Many of them were his people, and they held his hand and did what they could to ease his pains. There was nothing you could have done. Now come, please.

She walked off, her heavy boots thudding against the

ground. I followed, and she led me to a hut that was bigger than all the others. Inside, several women were around the large fire pit. Towards the back, where the shadows were deepest, I saw a figure lying on the floor and covered with a blanket. It was the Indian. He was still. His Coyote couldn't foil him anymore, and no more would his long, strange tales escape his lips. Through the loss of his stories, I wondered how many voices had been silenced. We approached the body.

—He spoke of you with hope, Levi said, squatting down near the body. —Or with enough hope that the native women convinced the rest of us that you should live, regardless of your decision.

—Decision? I asked.

—He swore you had already decided, she said, though she sounded unconvinced. —We let him think there was no question to that, because his time was near and it was best to let his mind be at ease.

—What are you talking about? I asked. But I had already begun to suspect exactly what she was asking me.

She reached under the blanket and picked up the buckskin bag that the Indian had carried since the day he came into my saloon. The bag that the Stranger had been seeking, ready to kill for. The bag that was still heavy with gold.

—But it can't matter anymore, I said. —The man who was chasing him, who wanted that gold, he's dead now.

She met and held my eye. —And yet the gold remains. As this man was passing, he had no wish but for you to finish taking all this gold back to the earth it came from.

—What business has a man like me got in returning it

to the earth? I am no mystic, and I don't pretend to understand the ways of the earth.

—You understand the ways of those who have poisoned
the earth, she said quietly. She held the bag out to me. As it
shifted, I heard the deadly clink of the soft metal inside. It
had once been nothing. Just part and parcel of the earth, a
piece of it like the rocks and the dirt. And then men like me
came along and declared it riches. And began to dig and tear.

The Indian had hoped his burden would be gone by the
time he reached where he started, where we were now. Yet
the bag was full. As I reached out, I felt its weight fall into
my hand.

—I'm sorry, I muttered to myself. To Joanna.

—Sorry is a beginning, Levi said.

I took her by the wrist. She let me hold her that way,
though I could feel strength in her arm and knew she could
have broken the hold whenever she wanted and reversed it
into something painful for me. Was that strength male?
Female? Something else entirely? Her face shifted. Or was
it his? I could not say.

—What are you? I asked.

—It is not because it is your world, Levi said, looking
me in the eye. —There is something more. A hesitation and
a shifting. Many cannot understand. And the ones who can
have known borders. Have known crossing and passing and
other. If there is a line, I am always on the far side, the wrong
side. With a smooth motion, she broke my hold on her.

Maria returned and took me back to the hut. I slept
most of the day, waking now and then to grasp at the buckskin

bag filled with gold. It was there, always near. It was my burden now.

Near sundown, Maria woke me and helped me up. I grabbed the bag and brought it with me as she led me away. There in the huge house, all the people were gathered. They picked up the mat the Indian lay on and took him out to the space in the middle of the houses. Then they lifted his body to the top of a tall pyre and set it there. The Indian women worked at the base of the pyre, building up the blaze. They were led by one woman slightly taller than the others, with jewelry of bones clicking at her wrists and around her neck, who they called Oya.

Soon the fire burned and leapt, rising and growing until it reached the Indian. His hair went up in a gust of flame. His ruined face disappeared behind the blaze. It was not long before it had obliterated him. Around the fire, the Indian women danced, each of them holding a feather up high as she circled the pyre.

That night we ate in the biggest house. First it was just Oya, then one by one the women brought food in baskets. As each handed over her basket, Oya took her shoulders gently, pulled her close, and kissed her forehead above and between her eyes in the spot I had first seen the Indian's wound.

Those around me tolerated my presence but mainly acted as if I was not there, talking and mourning amongst themselves.

Near dawn, most had departed the big house to sleep elsewhere. I was left with Levi once again. She seemed as a man and had remained that way all night. We did not speak until dawn began to pinken the sky.

—You must leave today, she said. —The women whose village this is have told me you cannot stay.

—I suspected, I replied.

The bag at my side was heavy. So heavy.

My beloved,

The road is long, and I have become quite lost on it. I have not been blessed with a letter of yours in some time, but somehow I do believe I sense your words. To hear or even read those sweet words plain would put my troubled mind at rest. For trouble is all around me and also within me. Perhaps if you knew these troubles, you would no longer hold me as dear as you always have. I pray that is not so.

Your figure recedes from my view. But never from my heart. I do not know when I will see you again. It may not be in this life. If that is the case, I wish as never before for the heaven you believe in. For a place where I will rest in your arms, with visions of this vicious world behind me. But I fear that even in some blessed afterlife, the horrors could never be wiped clean from my memory. This world is a demon and a devil, or, at least, it has come to be one. That much you know.

My burden is heavy. My path is dim. Perhaps there is a light at the end of it. Perhaps you wait in some quiet room, lit yellow and orange by a warm fire, and I will walk into that room and take off my hat, unbuckle my boots, and find rest for my weariness. Perhaps your gentle hands will undo all the wrongs. But are there any hands so strong, my love? Is there any fire so warm as to burn away all the slayings and the sins, the weaknesses and the wrongdoings? I do not know. But I imagine your hands so. That you could lay them quietly on my face, cover my eyes in warm darkness, let your soft touch flutter like bird wings. And in this darkness, all will become the innocence we have never known.

Good-bye, sweet beloved. The fire is low, and my burden is heavy.

Good night.